I was in it from the begin... that don't mean shit n... Break-beat House or wh... it before it metamorphosed into jungle. The one and ... Ragga Tekno, Jungle Techno, Ragga Jungle, Hardcore, Darkcore, The Dark Stuff, Ambient Jungle. All just labels to try and describe a feeling that transcends labels. Jungle is just something else. More than the sum of its myriad parts. It is the lifeblood of the city, an attitude, a way of life, a people. Jungle is and always will be a multi-cultural thing, but it is also about a black identity, black attitude, style, outlook. It's about giving a voice to the urban generation left to rot in council estates, ghettoized neighbourhoods that ain't providing an education for shit. Jungle kickin' ass and taking names. It run things, seen.

BACKSTREETS

Also in the BACKSTREETS series

SLACKNESS
BIG UP!
HERBSMAN

JUNGLIST

TWO FINGERS AND JAMES T. KIRK

BOXTREE

BACKSTREETS

First published in the UK in 1995 by
Boxtree Limited
Broadwall House
21 Broadwall
London SE1 9PL

10 9 8 7 6 5 4 3 2 1

Cover Art – Eddie Otchere
Cover Design – Martin Lovelock
Series Editor – Jake Lingwood

Phototypeset by SX Composing Limited, Rayleigh, Essex
Printed and bound in Great Britain by
Cox and Wyman Ltd, Reading, Berkshire

ISBN 0 7522 0603 6

A CIP catalogue record for this book is available
from the British Library

ALL NEW MINISTERS OF THE SUPER HEAVY FUNK

THE ALL NEW MINISTERS OF THE SUPER HEAVY FUNK would like to big up the World. All babies born feet first, the man like Eddie Otchere, Kofi, Jenny Baptiste, Mo, Lucia Fiore, Cyrill Brenya, Andrew Green, Dubious, Emile, Drew, Powermoves, Touch, Dirty Dozen and Muhammed Ali. The families of all, the Junglist's who keep it real and to every nigga working hard.
James T. Kirk

Dedicated to:

My Moms – you'll most probably never read this book and if you do, you'll most probably hate it. I love you and I ain't afraid to say it. My Dad, always there, we gotta get to know each other better. Bucky, look after yourself, I love ya. Rashana, Bucky's little bundle of joy, be optimistic. And finally *La Lune*, mistress of my heart, who showed me that feeling is a good thing. I ain't going no-where. Without all of you I wouldn't be the person I am, that you all know and love.

Big shout out to the Ministers keeping the funk alive in '95. That means you Elizabeth, Linda, Fazia, Matthew, Chris, Herbert, Cyril, and everyone that Kirk forgot. If you out there, don't worry we love ya!!

The TOUCH posse for putting up with us. To all those poeople who ain't afraid to go down – oral massive, you know it's da lick. The Jungle collective. The original drum and bass. If the music weren't there, this book would never have been written. Keep the Jungle real. No sell out.

And lastly, to the peoples out there. In the kingdom of the blind, the one eyed man is king. Peace to man, woman and child.

Two Fingers

Friday
The A-Side

"Jungle is a headfuck. The sound of a transformer banging its head against a wall."

Worries in the Dance

In the heart of the city's darkness, on the tarmac flyways and backways of London, crews from all sides, north, south, east, west, come correct for the gathering. They come ready and willing off the black streets to "Sarf" London, Elephant and Castle, looking for the future, searching for the riddim, the champion dub sound. Man, a man is geared up: Versace, Moschino, Ralphie, Armani, Paul Smith, name brands, cause the yout works hard for the money so now comes time to show and prove. Rudeboys burn hard; sparking up and passing it around, constructing the herd, 'cause man don't smoke solids.

As the car cruises through the city streets from its pick-up point, the Jungle builds up and gets louder, the bass speakers pop in the rush –

Check it, check it, the bwoy can't take it.

It's a whole new world under the cover of darkness, hiding from the beast, tuning up in anticipation of the dance. With flow of sound hanging thick in the air, crowding in and out of your lungs, becoming the oxygen you breathe, you realise that the youts in this for real. Red eyes and blunted, nappy headed and dreaded like the conquering lion of Judah, they be sinking deeper into the night ahead. Pulling up outside the Ministry, the crews make their way to the gate. Giving a nod to the security, the promoter, they breeze through. In this time man's paid his dues and as such people learn to free up with the freeness:

It's *the way . . . aright*.

Nothing is said as they move from house to car, from car to street, from street to jungle: a nod, a shifty grin, a gesture of gratitude and a passing of the spliff. With what's to come neither mind nor mouth is prepared. People work and rest, but never sleep, 'cause sleep is the cousin of death. They split as they enter the VIP lounge, kinetically sensing each other's movements and whereabouts as Craig and Biggie head for the bar as Q and Mr Meth move to the main arena slowly drifting into the darkness. Craig carries the Moët while Biggie handles the brandy, all the while surveying the heavily labelled crowd where nothing worn is cheap. As they walk like two mirrored dark-arse panthers, paralleling each other's movements, acknowledging the tunes and showing respect, they find a corner, away from the lights, where all the eye can see is mist and people, all the body can feel is the roll of the freight weight bass.

Q's stocky frame shifts to the corner, giving a nod to Craig: it's on. Following close behind were the Irish boyz. Tonight was simple, good times for all; a nod, the touch, the common greetings were exchanged and out came a matchbox. Craig took the box and in turn gave them a box of B and H. Each surveyed their contents and again a nod, the touch, the gesture of gratitude. Biggie took the box, carefully unwrapped the contents, rubbed it on the gum. The crew anticipated his reaction, the Irish boyz anticipated his reaction, his eyes scanned the crowd and he began to smile: *tings a gwon neatly*. The Irish boyz took the smile as a cue to leave and all was done. If God had made a better drug he kept it to himself, cocaine and weed would make most people's eyes bleed but these niggas came up hard, this was the way.

105.3 FM

I sit here in the sky, high above the clouds. Riding the microphone, lettin' it all hang out. My arse swingin' in the breeze. But you wouldn't know it, not in this leaky fucky of a skyscraper. Fuckin' 60s architects taking too much LSD and listening to the Beatles. Free love, free sex, tune in, turn off, drop out. 60s revolutionary bollocks, rebelling against nothing. All sound and noise signifying nothing. Middle class white trash copying America.

South London. It's my home. South London, where the estates grow lush and prominent, where the immigrants flow through. Now it's the Portuguese and the Somalians; who it was before, fuck knows, they've gone and all signs of them have gone with 'em. Pouring through and spreading out. Finding their niche in my eco-system. The South London eco-system. Streatham, Brixton, Dulwich, Lewisham, Battersea, Peckham, Herne Hill, New Cross,

Kennington, Putney, Croydon, Vauxhall, Elephant and Castle, Tulse Hill, Crystal Palace, Sydenham, Stockwell, Clapham, Balham, Tooting Bec. The names, the places roll off my tongue, the memories spill forth as they slide smooth into conscious being. So I give it loads and shout 'em all out.

This estate: whoever thought to put communities in these needles in the sky? These prisons of concrete and steel. These estates which were designed for vandalism, for holding your neighbours in contempt. That conduct sound. The doors which keep out no one. The windows that let in light but let out heat. The heating that doesn't work. The intense stink coming from every corner, of piss, staining each wall, marking territory. The ragged markings on the wall of the juvenile taggers, leaving their mark. Trying to give themselves a voice, an identity that is denied them by those who hold them in contempt. Waiting till it's dark so they can stand under lights, smokin', talkin', bonding . . .

They wait like predators, waiting, watching. Young and fierce. This is their time, their territory. The night belongs to them. It always has since the day they built these concrete monsters, these goliaths that split people, communities down the centre. Nowhere to play, nowhere to meet. Just live and survive.

But the estates are my home, where else can I go?

Look across, see Revolver hunched over the decks. Spliff hanging limply from between tight lips. End glowing. See his rolling equipment lying next to his stack of 12"s, white labels, dub plates, old, new and future imperfect. Headphone gripped between cheek and shoulder as his hands gently pull back, twist and turn over the Technics.

Pull the Marlboro Light out of its cellophane wrapping. Just like popping a virgin, opening a new pack of smokes. That knowledge that no one but you has opened this packet. That the first inhalation will be yours. I light the cancer stick with my Clipper. The good old Clipper, where would I be without you? Inhale, strong drag, suck it in, hold it down, let it run along my lungs, through those minute oxygen catchers. Let non-smokers rot in hell. Exhale, inhale, pretend I'm blowing smoke in Roy Castle's face. Long stream of cool greywhite vapour. Hold that lighted death dealer in my fingers, let the nicotine rush light up my neck and head, take another quick drag. Pull the mic close and breathe into it. Push up my levels and give the night its answer.

— 105.3 FM. The Style FM. Mage on the mic. The man like Revolver on the one and twos.

— *Do you know where your mum is at? Well I do, she's at my yard.*

— Live cusses on air. Coming atcha . . . Going out to the Muppet crew. The man like Big Bird, Ms Piggy, the man like Kermit, the man like Fozzie the bear. The whole Sesame Street massive.

— *Big shout to Jason, you muppet. Get that hand out of your arse and tell it to stop picking your nose.*

— It's the 0956, the 123, the 321. Cusses live on air come with them.

— *Michael, your mum's so nasty she ain't wash her pussy since you were born. You can still see the skid mark that your head left when you were coming out.*

— Last caller call back.

— *Caller from Kensington don't know whatcha chatting about, listen to some real Jungle. Big up your chest.*

— *Yo! Rupert, your neck back's so big that airplanes be mistaking you for Heathrow and trying to land on it.*

— Nah! Nah! That's just nasty. Rupert, you can't just sit there and take that, phone the 105.3 FM on the 0956, the 123, the 321.

— *Shout out going to the Earl's Court massive. All the Jungle crew. All the Bel Air crew.*

— Wheel! Wheel! My DJ ... Yes, here comes the rewind, back to the old skool for the Helicopter massive ... Move your wais, move your wais and feel the jungle lick your face ... Hol' tight the rest of the crew.

— *Last caller don't know what he's chatting about, don't know nothing at all. I ain't even gonna say nuttin'. Last caller wants to get a life and listen to some real Jungle.*

— You're in the zone with Mage and Revolver. Flexing on the S12s with the DJ Revolver.

Mr Meth

— **G**ive me dat phone. Jesus, I can't even use my own fucking phone. I got the living cuss.

Mercury One2One, the greatest invention since the vibrator. Ain't a black man seen without one. Press the call button and wait. Sit there half naked on the edge of my bed and wait, listening to the jungle pouring out of the speakers. It's silent as the numbers light up. Then I get put on call fucking waiting. Shit, I'm paying for this. I look at my little brother Elvin, with his little scrunched up face and that skinny coltish 12-year-old body. Just waiting to get to my phone so he can call his friends and chat about Nintendos vs Megadrive and their quick-flowering libidos. Grab him by his neck back and shove him out the door.

— An I keep telling you to stay out of my room, an' if I catch you using my phone again . . .

I leave the threat unsaid as I slam the door in his face and get his whiny voice out of my head. Still fuckin' call waiting. Loath to turn it off, the cuss that's in my head too good not to get out on air. BUT. The call's costing me big bucks. Slip my thumb over the arrow and press it. Disconnection. Push the aerial back down and put the phone back into the recharger with a practised flick of my wrist.

The full length mirror hangs on my wall, between posters of Michael Jordan and pictures of myself and the posse as we grow. Young faces in smiling repose as we stretch and grin for the camera. Look at myself then and now. The mirror Mum got me from some cheap secondhand place in Brixton. Then I saw the exact same mirror in Ikea to my everlasting shame. Ikea's for wannabe professionals, middle management and young up-and-coming professionals who ain't got enough money to buy quality goods at Habitat.

Look at myself in its flat reflective surface. Watch the muscles move under my skin, slide and move. Not bad, if I say so myself. Not bad at all. I'm no Schwarzenigga but hey, you make do with what you got. But I'm too fuckin' skinny. You know. I like to describe myself as slim, but muscular. Chocolate brown complexion, regular black features. My lips are too large and my nostrils rather wide, but I put two dogs in a bucket

FUCK IT. There's no point in being black if your lips aren't thick and full. Sensual, sexual, slip into that myth of black man as sexual animal, with an insatiable lust and a big black dick. Big like a baseball bat.

I scratch my nuts and feel my knob through my boxers. Most white women would be surprised. I look down at it lying there in its little nest of hair, dressing to its right. AHH! Just look at the cute little fella. Mum, can I have one, can I, can I? Please, I want a little penis. PLZ!

Run my hand through my non-existent hair. Bald headed just like Jordan, who adorns my walls. Jordan in flight, soaring majestically, body arching through the thin atmosphere. Is it a Bird? Is it a Plane? Is it Superman in black face doing an Al Jolson impression? NOO! It's Air Jordan flying through the air with the greatest of ease. I pick up the small basketball lying in with my dirty clothes at the end of my bed and start the running commentary, in a nasal commentator's growl.

— It's Jordan with the ball. There's 10 secs left on the clock. The Bulls down by 1 in the final quarter . . . Jordan fakes left, moves right, takes it inside. OH MY HE JAMMS! The Bulls win, the Bulls win. What a move by Jordan!

I stand and look around at the ball swinging in

the net. My room, my castle, my domain. Fuckin' tiny place, been in it for 14 years since my mum moved into the estate. Packed full of stuff, half of it hers. I'd need a room 3× as big to be comfortable. Not even enough room for a double bed. Rare is the time when girls have slept over, 'cause I'm a man who likes to sleep long and deep and awkward, not for me but for those who I sleep with. All sprawled out with my butt sticking out and taking up nuff space. 20-yr-old chest of drawers breaking down and holding too many socks. Clothes in the built-in wardrobe and my footwear by the desk that isn't used anymore except to be a table for the rising wall of books that sit on it. I love books, used to read 4 or 5 at the same time when I used to belong to a library. But more important than my books is my set.

My set all matt black and powerful, squatting beside my bed waiting to shit out powerful waves of sound. One thing I have to say about my room is that it has wonderful acoustics. It just brings the music to life. It took me 4 long months of heavy slog to buy it. Slogging in a friend's butcher shop. Hefting meat, smelling like stink 5 days a week, hands frozen, moving in and out of that fuckin' huge freezer, with those carcasses swinging like so much . . . like so much meat. It was enough to turn me into a vegetarian, well at least for those 4 months anyway. But I got it and that's all that matters.

Harman Kardon amp, Tannoy sixes, Marantz 62 CD player and Sony Tck570 tape deck (fuck a deck give me CDs). CDs and tapes lie across it, some in their case, some out of their cases, the CDs reflecting the soft light coming from my dimmed bulb. The speakers on their stands pump out a gusty wall of sound, driven hard by the amp. I reach down and feel the old bones creak and groan. I'm 21 and I'm falling apart already. 21 and don't know what to do with the rest of it, except buy clothes, music and go out. Dad keeps getting on my back about getting a proper job or going back into education, getting a degree. That if I don't do something he'll cut me off, stop giving me money, and for the instant he says it, it frightens me. Then I remember he's said it plenty of times before so why should now make a difference? – and blank it out.

I swirl the volume to the right and crank the sound even more, letting the sound run free. The bass rolls over me. Revolver's in the mix and he's throwing down some hardcore tunes. If they don't play tunes like this at the dance tonite I'm gonna cuss Craig, cuss him good. But that seems an obscure possibility as they have DJs in double figures: Slipmatt, Randall, Micky Finn, GrooveRider, Hype, Rizzla, Brockie, Devious D, GE Real and a whole heap of others all waiting to roll da beats.

Scratch my nuts again, feel the weight of my bollocks in my hand and give 'em a good old tug. Nod my head to the bass, jump up and wine up your wais. Feet lifting off the floor, knees coming high, the floor shaking as the bass runs through it. Runs and runs. Jungle. Jesus I don't know what I did without it. Jungle: it's a London thing.

Spray two deodorant on my armpit and splash some cologne on my neck over the sweat glands at the base of the chin. The cream runs smooth over my skin. Don't want any white elbows or knees, no skin flaking off in some girl's face. I like the feel of baby lotion all smooth and slick like sperm when you come over a girl's bottom and rub it in. Yeah, I like baby lotion. But the thought of coming over a girl's bottom depresses me for an instant, slips me into a down period. I have 'em on and off – anything can trigger them. They can last from a few seconds to a week, depends on how high I am emotionally at the time. Coming on girls' bottoms reminds me of Erika. She used to love it when I did it. I could come on her anywhere and she'd smile and rub it in, smooth her fingers through it. Used to say it was good for her complexion, her dark skin. Haven't spoken to her in ages. Hope she's alright. Last thing I heard, she was doing some business course as all black youth seem to do. *Do a business course and I'll succeed in the world*, which ain't saying shit. Think they're going somewhere 'cause they got an HND in business studies. Well, excuse me for dissing you but you can all suck my big toe. Caught up in that materialistic, capitalist *Got to get a BM to show everyone how much money I'm making. Carry me mobile phone round and when it rings speak real loud into it like it's something important.* Yeah, if you're so fucking important why you travelling on the bus for?

Now I'm angry and the music fuels it, slides into me and turns up the emotional intensity and I'm stamping on the floor as if to kill it. Letting the beat course through me, trying to do what those idiot white boys do and dance at 145 BPM instead of on the bassline. I ride high on the adrenalin rush for a few, then drop on to my bed, tired. Roll over and turn down the volume. Look at the watch on my wrist: wear it on the inside, be a real man. I've worn it like this for as long as I can remember. Seeing people wear it on the outside looks weird and I have to refrain from pointing my finger and yelling FREAK, FREAK.

Hope Q's on his way, he's usually on time. One of those be-on-time-my-life-depends-on-it types. Lie on my back and listen to the sirens wail, long and mournful. They scream of getting hook up, pulled over for doing nothing 'cept being black, oppression, riot gear and too much power held in mortal hands. Can't look 'em in the eye 'cause they'll hook you up. Lie and hear the sirens rolling closer. So loud, picture the white cars marauding through the darkness, blue lights spinning as they race down the streets looking for their prey. Hear them as they pass beneath my block, blue lighting up the night, overpowering the street lights. Then silence, that's what you call the sound of cars tearing down the road, children crying, people arguing, playing their music too loud. Noise crowding in, so loud that to think you have to write it down and then read it back to yourself to make sense of it.

Look at my watch again. Where's Q? Mum starts shouting at Bridget. Oh darling Bridget. Sister dearest! 17. I feel protective but she's an individual and as sexual as anyone else, and occasionally I put the hard heavy on some youth who's playing her, but generally I leave her to get on with her own life. All I can tell her is to steer clear of the bastards and not to get pregnant, life's too short to be getting pregnant at 17. I seen too many girls with child when they should be out enjoying themselves, living life to the full. She wants to come tonite, but I can't be dealing with anxiety over her and trying to find the honeys and enjoy the music all at the same time. Just let me do one thing at a time.

Look at my watch: still not here. Every stray noise is the lift stopping on our floor and Q stepping out. Hope he ain't got caught in a crash or nothing. He drives like a fucker, thinks he's indestructible once he's behind the wheel, and that shit heap his mum calls a car is a deathtrap. I don't know how it passes its MOT every year. I lie back and close my eyes, let the Jungle sweep me away onto other planes of existence, let it enter me like oxygen sustaining me, keeping me alive.

Ultramarine

*T*owards the sky I flew in a surge of tranquillity and found the unlimited existence in the shape of ultramarine and the my space was the only distance from me to knowledge, understanding and true freedom in peace: peace in freedom. The Earth disappeared as I flew and water, fire and air ceased to be. Life was not a dimension and I was not alive; I existed for the purpose of existence and it was this that taught me life. It taught me dimensions, and showed me the truth in the elements. Existence taught me freedom and peace, pure knowledge and tranquillity, she taught me ultramarine. She learned all this from me and we shared the blue until it was time for me to return to the imperfection and I fell up to the Earth with hope and remembering all I had learned, all I had taught. I found myself sharing the blue with other existers. We learned from each other and painted the Earth blue and it shone until the world took on the new form of ultramarine.

Q

Q's short and stocky with a neck 2× too big for him. He's into the perfect physique and all dat nonsense. Wants to be cut and ripped. Into discipline and denial. Forcing the body to bend to the mind's will. Apart from all of that my-body-is-a-temple bollocks he's OK. He's a friend. Smart and funny, in a caustic taking-the-piss way, but a little insecure (but aren't we all), over-compensating through the creation of this new image of his body. Think he's got a smell problem, washes like a nutter – and that big ass afro makes him look like a demon.

Open my eyes and he's leaning over me with his fingers stretching out his nostrils. Double take, almost shit myself. Yell, and then he's doubled over, clutching his sides like some demented hyena on speed, cackling like a witch, and when it hurts too much to laugh out loud, holding himself up by leaning against my wall, gasping out sobs, water streaming from his scrunched up eyes.

Q's got a weird sense of humour.

— So how you doing? Shit, you should have seen your face.

— Fine.

— HMMMM!

A companionable silence descends as I search for a top to go with the jeans and boots I'm about to pull on. I think I'm a bit of a closet biker, just need the Harley, the leather jacket and the dirty bandana wrapped around my forehead. Q's doing what all good black friends do, nodding his head to the music as he searches through my collection for something else to play. I could do a Craig on 'im and the old DJ bit, pulling out tunes one after another, playing 10 seconds of it before finding a next tune. But I'm hyped up, need to be moving on, getting out, doing things. Doing the mad goose juice. He's spread all over my bed like he's lived here all of his life. God, we are all so fucking similar yet dissimilar. Tastes in music, views on life, treatment of women. I don't know who I'd be friends with if I didn't have the posse. I've lost too many friends in the drift that comes when you leave school. You slide out of the fifth form, go off to college and lose 'em in the reshuffle.

They just slip away. The guys that you grew up with. The people you played patball with till it got dark, who you joked with on the school bus to playing fields out in the boonies – the only other time you saw grass apart from going into parks. The youths who rapped *Peter Piper* or *Bring the Noise* or RAW on those tubes back into school or to your gates. All in harmony, everyone knowing the words, Jason doing the human beatbox, verse after verse spitting forth. Not caring about the stares from the people sitting in their cocoons of silence; letting the sound venting from the lungs shout our defiance at them and their petty small-minded thoughts. The boys who you cussed with, fought with. Those who you envied and those that you admired and tried to be like. Trying to be confident with the girls as everyone shouted out, being suave sophisticated at 14. Being good at sports, joking and laughing or cussing and swearing.

But always growing, feeling yourself change and move, enemies becoming friends, friends becoming enemies. Hormones running wild but they're still your class, your rear. You knew them: Jason, Michael, Joe, Dean, Derek, Reggie, Morris, so many faces, personalities, and they're lost now. 5 years of space between who you were then and who you are now. Wonder whatever happened to them? Do they think of you as often as you think of them? Half remembering all that they represented, what they meant. The company they gave.

— Who's this? What's it sound like?

— What? Show it to me.

Q holds up a CD case. Swing group — 4 men talking about love and sex in sweet harmonies over a sample of a thick bass line.

— I don't know, bought 'em for my sister. She wants me to make her a swing tape.

Q looked dissatisfied with the answer, but I'm busy struggling with my pants. I hate it when clothes decide to take on a life of their own and spite you by making it impossible to put them on.

— Is Craig coming with us?

— I don't know. He broke up with Anna.

Struggle some more and pull 'em on, panting and gasping like I've just come.

— SHIT! When?

— A few weeks back, I think. He told me when it happened and I sorta forgot. He's hiding it, holding that shit inside. It ain't good for him. I tried to get him to get out – see the world again, show him it ain't changed – but he blew me out.

— Flav and Anna broke up. Shit!

The last expletive whispered softly and gently through half-open lips. Wonder. Craig and Anna, a couple if ever I saw one. They've been a couple for as long as any of us can remember. You know: LOVE! Full-on no-joke let's-get-married-and-have-a-house-full-of-babies love, love that wraps you up and don't let go. They were tied together on a molecular level, so close it frightened me. Entwined, up each other's arse. I've only been brushed by that sort of love and it frightened me into celibacy for a while.

Q grabs my phone and starts dialling like a madman.

— You got his mobile number?

— No, he only just got it.

He leans over and speaks softly into the phone, his voice slipping into telephone manner.

— Hello, can I speak to Flav? Sorry, can I

speak to Craig? This is Curtis, Mrs Langston. . . .
Me, I'm fine. Yeah, I haven't spoken to you in a
long time. . . . Yes I'll wait.

Chewing his bottom lip as if were bubblegum.
Q's the one who feels the most of us 4. The 4
musketeers, all for one and all of that.

— Yo Flav! How you been? Ain't talk to you in
a while, you know work and all dat. . . . Nah my
studies going fine, just a bit hectic at the
moment — you know, unitisation and semesterisation and all that shit. But that ain't what I
phoned to talk to you about. I just heard you and
Anna split. What happened? . . . Shit, that hard.
Look I know you want to be by yourself right
now, but being with people is better than being
by yourself. I don't want you to sit in your yard
and make tapes. . . . Yeah, hummmh. Don't worry
Flav I'll come round tomorrow. . . . Yeah I'm out.
Later.

Disconnection.

Craig's Obsession: 12 Inches of Plastic in a Quasi-Rotational Plane of Existence and a Parrot

I put the phone down and stare out of the window.

> *Mirror, mirror on the wall,*
> *Who's the fairest of them all?*

Sometimes I sit and watch the storm clouds roll across the sky. Grey and dark, the sky becoming a reflection of their grimness, their insubstantiality contradicted by the force that they herald. The storm an elemental part of nature. When the rain beats hard against the window pane, I watch my reflection and feel insignificant, the darkness of my skin no match for the darkness outside. The rain. My tears unshed. Watching myself crying, but not crying, for no tears run down my face, just my reflection's.

It sits there in its cardboard envelope, calling to me, whispering supplications in my ear. I take it gently in my hand, feel the slightly roughened texture of the cardboard at the edges, brush my fingertips over the smoothness of the illustration. Spin it between my fingers: slight fan of wind as it turns, stroking my cheek as if a caress. Read the notes on the bottom. Follow my finger, softly, inaudibly mouthing the words. Slip my hand inside and pull, ever so gently pull. Feel the paper slide out slow and easy. Cool against my palm. Aware of the weight of it within the fragility of its protection. Tip it on its side and let gravity slide it gently on to the fleshiness that is the base of my thumb. Balance it on the ball of that fleshy digit, letting my fingers rest on the silken circle, middle finger pressed against the hole of pleasure. Blow gently on it. My possession. The darkness, the blackness that is so much like me. Ebony. Cool. Mysterious, knowing. The light catching the grooves, raised ridges that spiral, spiral, spiral. Sound encased in plastic. I stare deep into the grooves trying to see where the sound emanates from, but it is beyond my view. I can only marvel at it, wondering at the magic that transforms the grooves into sound. Sound so perfect and clear in its intensity it captures my breath and robs me of coherent thought, making me nothing but a vessel for emotion as I spin 12 inches of magnificence between my fingers.

I sit hunched over on the edge of my bed, the arm balanced gently but surely in my fingertips, the needle fractions from the plane of existence that I desire to reside in. Let it slip quickly into the groove.

SOUND.

Stretch and turn the amp up, gentle increments of power until my room is throbbing with the sound. Until it blocks out all outside interference. No disturbances, no barking dogs or screaming kids: running, crying, playing, energy and vitality in every movement. No mothers pulling trolleys or pushing prams, each with a squeaky wheel and an attitude, irascible, loud, calling young kids to a halt: the hand descending, flesh reddening, tears welling. No buses or cars or motorbikes thundering down the road, engines roaring, tyres straining to keep contact and grip with the tarmac, bouncing through a pot hole.

Nothing but sound.

I would come and tape to the small hours of the morning. Tape after tape after tape, until sleep exhausted me and I would fall backwards onto my bed, listening to the hiss of the tape as it started.

The crackle of the needle in the groove. Then the sound would come, soft and deep, unforgiving in its intensity. Darkness surrounding me as the full sound took me away to sleep, perchance to dream.

Of parrots, more than the mind can count — parrots flying. Green, red, blue, yellow, crimson, orange, vermilion, indigo: a rainbow of parrots, a cacophony of parrots wheeling and soaring, straining to touch the heavens. And me tied to the earth, feet sunk in clay, base and foul. Never able to be one of the feathered few. Only allowed to watch and know the joy in my mind but never to experience it in my heart. Parrots who were the sound made flesh, not subject to the limitations of men, not subject to any law man has created for they are above our petty laws, they are above everything and anything.

I would wake then. Lying still and silent, listening to the faint hum coming from the amp, amplified and reaching me through the speakers. Lie and feel the tears run softly down my cheeks.

My mother comes up with these small pearls of wisdom, ingrained in her by her mother and her mother before that. Gems like If *you haven't got horse, ride cow* or *Don't step over someone when they are sleeping or they won't grow*. To me they are insignificant. What do I care about cows and horses. I'm a child of my time. I know Sega, Nintendo, separate systems, Apple Macs, SL 1200s, MTV, soundbites, action replays, digital sound, interactive multi media, virtual reality. I live in a world where science fiction is out of date because science fact is outstripping it. Where what we imagine today is reality tomorrow. But for all this I still have to live my life and know that to be an individual is essential, but that for me to feel complete I must (it is a social imperative) bond with someone else. Male or female, depending on my sexual preference. Sometimes I wish I had stayed 6, then I wouldn't have to deal with this. This heartbreak, this confusion, this pain.

> *Don't walk away boy,*
> *Our love won't hurt you,*
> *So what you say?*
> *Don't walk away boy,*
> *I'll be right there for you.*

Female voices in unison soaring, rising. Taking my heart and soul with them. The harmony frightening in its virulence, the case with which it can take me with it. The sound overwhelming, a bright light after years of darkness, blinding in its intensity. I take the needle out of the groove and place it in its holder. Look around me as if for the first time.

My room strange as if it belongs to someone else. The clutter of it, clothes thrown across the floor, trainers and worn socks lying together beside the closed door, puffer hanging over the chair. My room dominated by the four floor-standing speakers and the long rows of records against the wall. My system at the edge of the bed, dusty but constantly in use. My bed rumpled and crumpled, the quilt in a heap at the corner. The walls covered with photos and magazine covers, images cut off half frame, quarter frame; tickets from the cinema, an index to what I've seen over the years. Tickets and flyers for concerts and club nights. Jazz Cafe, Maximus, the Fridge before it went gay, Brixton Academy, Iceni, Fresh n Funky, Leave My Wife Alone, Funkin Pussy.

I rub my eyes and scratch my bollocks, looking down at the stiffness lying against my stomach. Ignore it and head to the toilet for a slash. Mouth feels dirty and nasty and I don't want to go anywhere, but I brush my teeth anyway and stand looking in the mirror. Staring, staring, staring, trying to see what I like about myself, what anyone would like. Try to smile. Stop, it doesn't make me look any better. Rub my hand across my face, place my forehead against the cool surface for a moment and wonder why the world was designed the way it was. Who wins? Who loses? Who cares? I retire to my room, closing the door quietly behind me.

*

The door opens quietly and I smell Anna. Soft intoxicating flower smell. I remember when it used to cover me, envelop me. When her tongue used to flick my nipple and I used to gasp aloud, how she would laugh deep in her throat and encircle it with her mouth. I turn over and look at her standing in my doorway. Is she uncertain? I don't know? I let the silence stretch and stretch, just looking at her, my head resting on my arm. I sit up, pulling the quilt about my waist and still the silence stretches between us like some umbilical cord connecting us. I bend down and search briefly through the tapes at my feet, find the right one, slip it into the deck and listen to the sound boom out. Militant. Turn it down so that we can talk over it, but the silence is still there. I grow weary of it and start the conversation.

— So. Why are you here?

— I came to see how you were.

— You could have phoned – you know my number.

— You know I hate mobiles, and I can't stand that damn message you've got on yours that I always get 'cause I can't get through.

— Sit down. You're making me nervous.

— No I can't, I'm not staying long.

— If you're not staying long, why did you bother coming?

— I came to get my records.

She took a deep breath before she said this. I can feel the blood rush away from my head, sense the spots at the edge of my vision, the coldness of my crown. My mind swims. It's hard to concentrate, to think logically, my brain feels like it's shutting down. Then it's gone and I can see clearly again. I take in a slow juddering breath and look at her, look through her, my mind gone blank. Gone to the null place in my skull, where it is still taking information but just isn't using any of it. I can think on anything, everything. Set my mind free to go on any tangent, not knowing for how long it will last but enjoying it nevertheless. It always used to frighten her, unnerve her when I did this. Reminding her of when her cat died and how it stared unseeingly at her for hours, its head next to hers on the pillow she was sleeping on, only for her to wake and stare deep into its eyes, reach out to stroke it and find it stiff and cold.

I blink and come back to myself. Blank experience No. 72 over.

— You came to get YOUR records?

— Did I stutter?

— Which ones?

— Stop playing games, you know which ones. Mary J. Blige, Jodeci, Marvin Gaye, I Want You, Aretha Franklin, Young Gifted and Black, Sade, Intro, Pharoah Saunders, Donny Hathaway, Bill Withers, Anita Baker. Do I need to go on?

The names roll around inside my head and I look at my collection, seeing all the records I've taken from previous girlfriends, know which columns they're in and how many times I've used them to complete a tape. My hands move swiftly, going through the records I have amassed in my 20 years of life, the weight of them pressed against my knee as I crouch over them, pulling them out and laying them to one side. Shifting from column to column, repeating my actions until 24 records lie on the floor beside me. I tidy my collection and stand, hearing my knee joints crack, my back strain. I stand in front of her and wonder whether I should ask for my bag back, that she wears so proudly. Could I be that petty?

As she loads the records into her bag I watch the tattoo that she always said was a phoenix, but looked more like a parrot to me, moving as the muscle moves beneath the skin. Skin so soft that even now I desire to place my lips upon it. Touch it, know that it is mine. Possession is 9/10 of the law.

Turn away. Watch the rain playing upon the window, try to concentrate on it as she places herself against my back, warm and soft, kissing me gently on my neck. Feel myself stiffen. Then she is gone and the rain streams down the frame, the scent of her sharp in the air and against my skin.

The record sings to me as I ease it from its sleeve and I place it down gently and begin the automatic ritual of turning on my system. Push in the power button on the amp, see the green light come on around the button as the electricity rushes into it, electrons alternating, positive–negative, positive–negative, positive–negative. The short pause as the amp powers up and the slight inrush of air as the speakers come up to speed. Move my hand up to depress the switch for the tape deck, see the luminous back behind the tape light up, the LED display come to life. Open it, hear the soft whirr of motors as the door slides forward. Take out the tape and wind it on with my little finger until the dark magnetic strip is ready before putting it back and hearing the motor whirr again, pussycat soft, as it closes. Pick up the record and slip it on to the solid silver spike, letting it drop featherlite down onto the slipmat, giving it a little spin before bringing the deck up to speed.

33rpm I think. Lift the needle, bring it across, smooth, gliding, frictionless, cue it up and then let it delve into that 12 inch plane of existence.

Sound erupts from my speakers, an overwhelming tidal wave of sound. Concentric circles of force move backwards and forwards, throbbing in their cases. Put the deck onto record mode, check the levels, tweak it up a bit, a bit more. Yeah that's good. Cue the record again, let my finger tap the record button and . . .

> Baaaaaaaaaaaabee!
> I'm hot just like an oven.
> An'
> Baaaaaaaaaaaabee!
> I can't go much longer,
> It's getting stronger and stronger,
> 'Cause when I get that feeling,
> I want sexual healing.

Original Nuttah

The cold multitude of the street life comes to a dead stop in the vast concrete towers of the city. The ebb and flow of life ends in the exit of the jungle; within that enclosed infinity the mists of human uprising flow like the locks on a dread. The flesh, the crowd, it's all memories in the back of a car; in the streets no one cares if you scream.

As the Mercedes glides through the city from Elephant and Castle towards Dalston, the Irish boyz rest themselves, staring at the spotless streets of barriers, the stars, the cleaners getting off night buses, the police on the lookout for terrorists and black kids riding from one ghetto to another. Up through Bank, past Liverpool Street, past radication packed like dogs, ready to beat up and kick up the yout in their vans. In the hope of reaching sanctuary soon, they speed through the city. Coming up to the traffic lights at the top of Old Street they speed a red light turning amber.

Now, four boys in a Mercedes estate, smoked up windows, pumping deep Hardcore was enough to make them pounce. By the time they reached Dalston, time was up. It was hello like before.

As the policeman calmly walked up to the car, the boy they called Shawn lost it. Too much speed, frustration, fear, whatever – he just blew. As raddie leaned into the window Shawn said, as thick and as fast as his accent could spit:

— Get the fuck outa here and gimme a ticket.

— Excuse me.

— I didn't do nothing wrong. I know what's goin on, you're fuckin' with me 'cause I'm Irish.

By this time everyone was in shock and was trying to sneak out of the car.

— I know I was speeding but I had to get my dog some food.

The policeman's reaction was to stay calm and not react. He slowly pulled out his notebook and began to take notes. Shawn was wired like a bulb, buzzing hard, but the policeman didn't seem to respond.

— Go fuckin' pick up some criminals and stop working people driving like myself. I was only doing 55 in a 60 zone and I saw a saying 40.

Everyone in the car began to panic; they were carrying weed, pills, H, rock, uppers, downers, the works. And Shawn was babbling to a policeman. One of them began to explain:
— Sir, we're sorry, if you can . . .

Shawn began the engine.
— What the fuck ya doing, Shawn?

— I know, I know, I've been done for speeding before. You do it, you get caught, you get the fine and you hope you don't get caught. And I was doing fine till I met him.

— Ah fuck off Shawn and shut up.

The policeman interrupted.
— Excuse me, sir, let me explain.

At this point it was amazing how the policeman was still calm, sounding like some nonce in playschool.
— Alright then. The green copy is for your records, sir. The blank spaces you fill and return within 28 days; read the instructions on the back.

Attached is an envelope. I hope you can afford the stamp because the fine's probably goin' to be £1000.

This caused a epileptic reaction. Shawn began to scream.
— Are you fucking crazy? You fucking mother cunt! Jesus cunt Christ! OH ... OH ... OH ... My dad's car.

By now everyone was holding Shawn down.
— You fucking crazy? £1000? I wasn't speeding. I've never heard of a fine like that, you fucking imbecile.

He began to tear up the piece of paper and threw it on the floor.
— Excuse me, sir, if you don't pick up this litter you've made I'll fine you for littering.

— You fuckin' cunt!

And he jumped out picked up the papers. As the boyz watched in disbelief the officer told them to move on, Shawn still screaming and cursing. Then he reversed the car, put it into drive and ran the policeman into the ground. This had the effect of shooting the pope. Out of

every nook and cranny came very sort of policeman on earth; out of nowhere came sirens and
the beast.

Red Eye

*Me-t-h-o-d Man . . . Here I am,
Mr Meth, the Method Man.*

It's not until I'm in the car and strapped in with Q pulling Gs trying to take his mum's beat up Cortina into the stratosphere and from there to the farthest reaches of space, and I sit there like Picard from *Star Trek* feeling like saying E*ngage* (but Q ain't into *Star Trek* so he wouldn't get the association) that I remember that I'm out of blow. The yell's ripping out my throat and I'm screaming like a demented child who's been denied his ice cream. Yelling and kicking, cursing heaven and hell. Q's seen me like this before and he doesn't bat an eyelid. I've got my Rizlas, my lighter, some Silks in my pocket, but no fucking gear. Shit! How could I be so stupid? I knew I should have bought some more. Q won't have none, his body's a temple and my irrational, transparent desire for the dreaded weed comes under his continued contempt. But he lets it slide as long as I don't blow smoke in his face.

Craig might have some but what I've seen of him lately ain't inspiring no confidence. He looks mash up, totally and utterly. Biggie'll surely have some. He's a top-of-the-line dope fiend. Me and Biggie get on fine. I hate being in a dance and there is no chance, not even a smell of getting a puff, unless you look like some poor ass nigga looking to blag some off people you don't know. Because you know when you don't have any everyone else'll be drowning in the stuff. The air'll be thick with that hard pungent smell that slides up your nostrils and dances along the back of your throat. You can smell it and feel it and your mind slips into that blowback frame of mind. When it starts to hallucinate and reminisce over what it's like to get stoned. Stoned, high, blunted. When you drag deep and the top of your head goes cold and light and you just feel like nothing can touch you. That if you had the chance this is the way you would feel all the time. This state between conscious thought and unconscious being. Light and strong, powerful yet inert. Just damn mellow. When the beat's rolling as you drown in the wave of bass, letting it wash you where it will, then the spliff glows red in your fingertips and you don't need anything else. Free up with the freeness.

When I was 16 and clean living – no smoking, no drinking, no sex and definitely no drugs – there were 3 youths in my year who would smoke all the time. Smoke and smoke, till their eyes were red raw. The joke was that every time a teacher would ask where they were (when they'd be puffing away in the back field) we'd say that they were catching the red eye. They used to puff hard and vigorously and every time I'd see them I'd wonder what it was like. Will I cough? Is it rough on your throat? How long do I inhale for? Questions spinning in my head, like a cannon about to explode, all you needed was to light the fuse. All night you'd see the red glow illuminating them as they stood under some trees by the gate. Smoking till they were red eyed and senseless. I used to catch the same bus as them and they'd always burn at the back. There it was. On the back of the 133 going to Brixton Craig, Q and Biggie casually brought me in – and now I smoke up storms like the Method Man.

Legitimise now so I can stop getting hassle from the radii. I remember when I was in Amsterdam. They didn't haul you up over there. Me and Craig we'd sit in the café and smoke like there was no tomorrow. Sit there puffing on these fat ass candlestick spliffs, getting stoned off the planet, then rushing to gulp down litres of orange juice when the urge for munchies was upon us, our taste buds dry and parched after that heavy session. Then it'd be off to the nearest porno theatre to catch a few flicks. When I came back I was deep into nasty sex. Riding a woman hard, not caring, out to hurt her. Ramming into her like no man's business. It got on top of me for a while, all the stuff I'd been trying to hold inside, just came out in a rush. My brush with love opened me up to an emotional minefield and I couldn't handle it. Fuck I'm getting maudlin. Next thing I'll be crying in my beer and saying:

— I wuz robbed, man. Robbed of my youth, my energy, my life.

I look back into myself and see how my train of thought has moved from one peak to another trough, and I'm not going to let it get in my way. Pull myself together, back from the brink of the abyss of depression and look past into the night, my saviour. Watch the night stream past the window, my cloak, my saviour, hiding me from those that would oppress me. Look up, crane my neck to see the moon, *la Lune*, mistress of the night, see her slip behind a bank of clouds, then reappear in all her majestic glory, full and potent — no illusion.

Silence reigns in our car. Q's concentrating on his driving, even though he's trying not to let it show – tongue sticking out of the side of his mouth, his brow furrowed. The only time he doesn't look like he's concentrating is when he's talking to you or listening to music. I sit back and look again out of the windows. People on the streets, walking up and down, moving, talking, interacting. I turn on and feel the car jump around as the bass rolls free. An old 70s cortina straight out of *The Sweeney*, behaved like a Low rider.

— Sound, Bwoy.

Revolver

I was in it from the beginning. Just a yout back then but that don't mean shit now. Back when Jungle was still break-beat house or whatever the fuck you wanted to call it before it metamorphosed into Jungle. The one and only. Ragga Tekno, Jungle Techno, Ragga Jungle, Hardcore, Darkcore, The Dark Stuff, Ambient Jungle. All just labels to try and describe a feeling that transcends labels. Jungle is just something else. More than the sum of its myriad parts. It is the lifeblood of a city, an attitude, a way of life, a people. Jungle is and always will be a multi-cultural thing, but it is also about a black identity, black attitude, style, outlook. It's about giving a voice to the urban generation left to rot in council estates, ghettoised and neighbourhoods and schools that ain't providing an education for shit. Jungle kickin' ass and taking names. It run things , seen.

I was there when Rave just went too fast. So

fast that unless you were taking elephant size wraps you weren't gonna dance to shit and my friends would drag me to rave after rave after rave and I'd stand up and screw my face, until they played two little tunes with a Ragga sound and I'd jump up with the sound until it disappeared. Then Hardcore went underground and I went with it – went underground and evolved into Jungle – and all the ravers that were into Hardcore slid into happy House or back to their Garage roots. Back to that false high, that false hope. That false love when you're EEEEing off your face and then tripping off your nut and the music goes:

DUFF!
DUFF!
DUFF!
DUFF!

When you love everyone and everyone's your soulmate, the closest person to you in the entire universe. Arms flying, elbows swinging. All feet stamping on the DUFF! All the people into it. Eyes wild, smiles strapped to their faces. House: that middle class bullshit. So boring and predictable, so irredeemably foul in its twisting off the bassline, turning it into that abomination of a metronome. A black music form watered down and turned into an acceptable, even positively welcomed form. Taken over by those who desire to have music that they can dance to and always look like they have rhythm. House – I hate to say it, I sound like my mother – but it sounds like so much fuckin' noise. I stand in there and it turns my heart cold, my face screwed up, my body still, feeling the melody wanting to take me up and away from this purgatory. But it can't, it can't get past the bassline. My mind – and so my body – refuses to let it flow through me. Like a rock in the surging waves, letting it all just run past, leaving me smooth and unruffled. Not to say I haven't enjoyed a House rave. I have, but then I've been speeding like the proverbial nutter. I've never liked the knowledge that I have to take a drug to enhance my enjoyment of music and make myself want to dance. To enjoy myself I have to take E or Speed or a bit of a Trip or all of the above.

I like to smoke, who doesn't? But pulling on the herb is mellow, more likely to get you to sit down than to dance all night. So I'm caught in the middle with friends into a sound and a scene that ain't saying shit and saying:

— We can't dance to Jungle.

— It's too fast.

— It's just fucking depressing.

— It's a noise, just noise. It sounds like a fucking Techno.

— We don't like the atmosphere.

— All those Raggas.

Meaning there's too many black people there. I don't take it personal, it's just what they've been socialised into thinking; one black person might be alright but a mass dance and all that dark, depressing, dangerous black music? No way, not this boy.

House is a false sound, a false consciousness, a false sense of reality. The people who listen to it, enjoy it and dance to it want to lose their worries and fears in the mere act of dancing. But Jungle's truer to humanity's real roots. It cuts away the falseness, gives you the ups and the downs, the dark and the light. White is good, black is bad/evil. Therefore House is good and God and Jungle is bad and dark. The dark forces of those Jungle bunnies come to get us. Anything that involves more than one black person, that is aimed at other black people, is inherently dangerous. Because it hasn't been reconstructed and regurgitated for the white mass culture. Top of the Pops. Imagine every pop tune of the next year coming with a Jungle mix. White wash.

But I ain't bitter, so I let it go 'cause I always wanted to be a DJ. You know, dictate what people listen to, make them listen to what you like, and then they like and listen to what you listen to. That's the major thing, getting others to love and dance to what you love. But it's not only that but also the actual act of DJing, the technical skill that you have to acquire to be any good. Being able to mix, to scratch, to know which song to put where and how to keep the crowd reaching for that space, that place where you feel you could dance forever and never stop.

My job is to make the music as seamless as possible, so that it seems as if every song was made with the specific purpose to be played after the one before. Basically I'm here to make the crowd forget I'm here, to disappear from their conscious thoughts. The only time people know you exist is when you fuck up or when they hail for the rewind after you drop some roughass tune. The first you pray never happens. The second you wish could happen all the time. That's why you practise. You want that feeling of elation when the hands go up and the yells and the whistle surrounds you and everyone's screaming for the rewind. That's what you go out and spend big amounts of money on records for.

So I drop the needle into the groove, hand on the disc, pull it back, slide it forward, fingers taut but relaxed as well. Practice has made me nonchalant, devil-may-care. Stand there feet apart, weight balanced as I lean, head clamped to my neck, the slim body of the phone between shoulder and head. Hear the soft sounds of the other record coming through, change the pitch, slide it with my nail, watch the green light flicker then fade away. The flowing light defining the deck as it spins, black digits blurring into one long line. Switch the record, lift, spin it quickly, slip it back on. Needle into the groove. Windows closing, closing; change pitch, shift back, once . . . twice, beat on beat, find the right moment. Slam it. Quicksilver movement of the wrist and it's in, the beat is booming. Jungle.

Conversations in a Vacuum

Sitting to the side of Q. The night sailing past, the bass booming around us. Watch the kerb. I'm screwed up tight in my seat, trying not to yell out as the car thunders around corner after corner. Q with his hand at the top of the steering wheel, pretending he's one of the Dukes of Hazard or dreaming of being Nigel Mansell. His foot hard on the accelerator, pushing the car really hard. So he's got a licence, but he's not insured on the old dear's Cortina. She takes it on faith that he drives like she does, very slowly and carefully. I've got a licence. OK, if I took my test I'd have a licence, but I've been driving for as long as I can remember. Well, as long as I can remember since I was 12. To take my mind off the fact that Q could kill me at any moment – and me having dirty underwear on. Mum's always telling me to change 'em. "Put on new underwear, if you have an accident I don't want the doctors seeing your dirty drawers and making me ashamed." When she says this she also pulls out Grandma being ashamed when Grandad had his stoke and was taken to hospital; rather than remembering the pain and grief that she felt, all Granny can remember is the dirty pants that they pulled off him before they operated on him. Got to drag my mind off that thought. Not my dirty underwear, but slamming into another car at upwards of 50 mph. What to do, what to do? With nothing else in the air I start a conversation.

— So who you going out with now?

— Her name's Emily.

— White or black?

Q looks at me hard. I smile: I like getting under his skin. And hey, you gotta know these things before events start taking on a life of their own.

— She's black.

— With a name like Emily? No way. Pure middle class white trash, I can smell it. Like bacon.

I start sniffing like a pig and Q's foot just twitches on the accelerator, taking us just below 60.

— Her name's Emily Ngowurah, she's Nigerian.

Sharp intake of breath: Nigerian, slippery territory here, how to navigate it? I'll just kick in the front door like I usually so.
— Nigerian. Dodgy, very dodgy, heard bad things about 'em.

— Don't even start. I don't want to hear some long-winded rant on the merits of Amazonian women over Nigerian women, OK.

I pause: pretend like I'm gonna let it go.
— OK, so describe her to me. Short, tall, thin, fat, big breasts, wide nose? Come on, tell me.

— She's nice looking, very nice.

— Fuck nice, describe her in intimate detail.

Q leaves a gap in here as if he's thinking. I know he's just trying to fool me into shutting up so I ask the question he knows I'm always gonna ask any of the crew.
— She giving you any?

— I ain't answering no coarse question from you.

— Coarse? What's coarse about it? I just want to know if you diggin' it. How long you being going out with her?

— About a month.

— A month and you still ain't getting any? You slippin'.

— Like every girl you go out with you fuckin' like rabbits on the first date?

— Yeah, of course.

I laugh. I know it's absurd and so does he. Girls ain't down for that unless you're Biggie. Girls be throwin' their panties at him, like confetti.

— OK so I ain't Mr Casanova sex god himself, but it's fun to dream. So why ain't she giving you any?

— I'm not discussing my sex life with you.

— Oh you gettin' all uppity on me. You sure ain't gettin' none. So if you ain't gettin' none, I suppose she ain't licked it yet.

— Fuck you. All the time you be going on about pussy this and pussy dat. Gettin' pussy, licking pussy, banging pussy. Do you think about anything else?

— What else is there to think about? Do you ever think about Caz?

He's gone deep there and I've got to pause to compose myself. I try not to think about her too much, it still hurts. Breaks me up and I can feel the tears hot and wet at the back of my eyes, that clogging feeling in my throat. Cassie of the soft hair and the all-enveloping love. I hurt her so many times trying to love, trying to be with her. I let it go and bring myself back to the conversation at hand. Q thinks he broken free, but I rope him back in with another subject he ain't too quick about answering on.

— So if you ain't getting any, you wanking then?

— What is it with you? I do not wank. I have never wanked, will never wank. Save the seed.

— Fuck all of that eastern philosophy. If she ain't giving you none it's back to the old five knuckle shuffle.

— No discipline, no self-control.

— Oh give it up, wanking's as natural as breathing. You wake up, you wank, you get out of bed feeling good and go about your day. Wanking's a natural release. Nothing nasty or perverse about it.

— If you ain't got it in your hand, you're trying to get it into a girl's hand. All that time you spend wanking you could be out doing something useful.

— Something like what, signing on the dole? Go on tell me, be my mother.

— Go back into education, get a degree, get a job, earn some money instead of just spending it. You've got a brain: use it.

— All I want is a conversation and I get a sermon from Q The Pious.

— You can't censor what I think and you asked me to tell you so I did.

Silence reigns again. Q's driving silent again. His face screwed up. I'm hunched in my seat watching him, watching the road. This is supposed to be a fun weekend. Party all night, party all day. Get blunted, if I can get some gear, and watch the honeys wack up their wais. I could be proud and let the silence stretch and stretch and stretch. Taut and pregnant. But I hate those, when everyone's in the car sitting in silence just watching the lights go by. So I break it.

— We're supposed to be enjoying ourselves. I didn't get into this car to argue with you. I got in this car so we could pick up Biggie and go listen to some Jungle. Agreed?

— Agreed.

So saying, I turn up the volume again to make talking impossible unless you're telepathic, and let the bass flow pure and free like mineral water. Watch out world, here we come. Ready or not.

Biggie

When it come
It coming like a bloodclot heart attack.

I turn down the radio. Locked into 105.3. Let the words flow over me like a gentle summer breeze. I'm the perfectionist. I create perfection. Perfection is all around me. To achieve perfection I buy quality goods. Goods that last forever. None of that shite cheap stuff. Just 'cause it costs a pound don't mean you have to buy it. Go with-fuckin'-out, that's one of my mottoes. If you don't have enough money, deny yourself. Wait. Wait until you do, then you buy it. Get the best. The best is always in short supply and when it is available it costs more than you can afford. So I sit and wait. Just like the old man in kung-fu movies. Sitting and waiting for some young beaten-upon schmuck to come over and say *Master teach me*. Then I awake, crawl forth from my shell and teach. Show the youth of today what it takes. And you know what it takes, it takes perfection. Technique. In the end it all comes down to technique. If your technique is weak you are not going anywhere. Technique is all. Only through technique is perfection attained.

How do you write your name, hold a pen, put on your clothes? Break a movement, an action, down into its component parts. Find the most efficient way between those points. The smoothest route, the route which takes the least energy, the least effort, the route that looks good. Combine them and you have perfection. Only through a breaking down of components to their basic parts can you find out how to achieve alignment. The beginnings of perfection. Perfection in all its many forms. That is what I strive for in everything I do. Perfection. Write it down see how the letters form to make that single solitary word. Perfection.

The Japanese know about perfection, about breaking down a movement and then recreating it into a ritual where every action has meaning, has power. About how all things have an innate beauty, how each movement becomes in and of itself a beautiful thing if done correctly. How perfection is attained through the simple things, the simple actions and the simple thoughts.

I sit in front of my stash, my resin. My fingertips brown from rolling the resin between them.

Know deep in my being that I want to make another piece of perfection and through the creation of another small piece of perfection become perfected in the making. I pull out the Golden Virginia, sitting cross legged, calm myself, slow my breathing, slow my heartbeat. Feel my heart slow and in the slowing become one with my blood, become my blood. Just another corpuscle flowing through my veins, bouncing around within my arteries. Put the skins in my hand, fold half way, nod my head to the beat. Tongue smooth and divine, lick along the folded edge. Tear: feel the wet paper pull apart in my fingers. The light dims as I lick another gummed edge and place it on to my Rizla, extending it. Know my place in the whole structure of the universe, within things seen and unseen, known and unknown. Let it lie there in front of me. Lighter held at the ready as I contemplate the paper waiting to be filled: white now, just empty. Waiting. Thumb rolls along the steel wheel, spinning it. Spark, ignited the gas, the fluid. Flame. Prometheus chained to a rock for giving flame to humanity. Golden orange, glowing, illuminating my face, my eyes, my skin. Hold the lump above it, warm it, feel it go soft and malleable. Crumble it, break it down into its component parts, into smaller lumps, granules. Brown resin-stained fingers rubbing the resin.

Rub it, light it, warm it, rub it. Every action smooth and slow, a ritual in the little things. Place it within the envelope: it falls like snow, light and weightless. I look into it and become part of it, falling into that brown heaven, that soft pungent smell rising to my nostrils. Inhale deep and pungent sensi. Feel how it slows down my world, my life. Coat the inside of that envelope with my brown perfection. Pull out the tobacco and line it sparingly. Don't use Silk Cut. Burns the fuck out of my throat. All cigarette tobacco is harsh. Bends reality to its own making. Bends reality to a design which I haven't drawn, so I repudiate it. I don't smoke if it's been rolled with Silk Cut, Marlboro Lights or any other cigarette. It's an invasion of my perfection. Pull the tobacco out strand by stand, feel it soft and moist in my fingers. Just like pussy. Pussy smells like hash to me, dark and moist. Soft and juicy. Pull the half finished joint to me, pull it close, hold it, roll it, using just the tips. Once, twice, three times. Hold it between forefinger and middle finger and let my thumb roll it upwards. Tongue out, supplication, slide it sensuously along the gummed edge. Fingers rolling it closed, sliding along it, wrapping it tight. Tear the card, pull it between thumb and forefinger, slide it in, feel it hold. A nice long roach. Wrap the end and wait. It lies there in front of me, my perfection. Each movement smooth oiled, done without thought. Done instinctively as if breathing. I contemplate it, feel the release. Know my perfection is attained through this one act. Leave it there as I stand, push up my lighter and dance, illuminating myself with my lighter, the flashes sharp and bright. Feet stepping higher, mouthing the words.

— *We're not gonna die, we're gonna get outta here.*

Turn around and see my perfection, pick it up and light it. Swift effortless motions, dragging it in deep into my lungs, feel it rushing, rushing, that languid effortless underwater feel coming over me, encompassing me, taking me back to the womb all warm and secure, another larger heartbeat in synchronisation with mine, dreaming of a world unknown and unseen.

— *I don't want to die. You're not gonna leave me are you Ash?*

— *Not while I'm smoking Mary.*

Perfection. Just call me perfection.

Jap's Eye

A Shock for Mr Meth

— **W**hat do you mean you went for an AIDS test?

I'm sitting in Biggie's kitchen, the smell of food wafting around. Q's hunting around opening cupboards and generally acting like a nigga as he hunts for sustenance. Right now I'm in shock, shit's happening that's out of control, teetering on the brink of Armageddon, AIDS tests, shit, we're young, immortal. So now you have to wear an overcoat but if it means living another day I'm all for it.

— I went for an AIDS test. Shit was worrying me.

Biggie's small, maybe 5'5" possibly 5'6", with his cute face and laughing eyes. A tight taut body, with large hands and long workman fingers, heavily callused. He's sitting slumped in a chair, his hands making shapes in the air as he talks, wandering on into territory only his mind can see. A wide mouth with thick lips that we tease him about. A mouth that is set in a cocky grin as he fields our questions about the intimate details of his bodily functions.

— He's an adult, he can make his own decisions.

Q sticking in his two cents' worth. I'm just trying to work shit out and people keep jumping down my throat.

— Fuck that!

— Fuck you!

— No, fuck you! That's some serious shit you jumping into.

— I know what I'm doing. I just want to be sure.

— Sure that your dick wouldn't fall off in your hand.

— Seriously.

— Never seriously. No, not seriously.

— I just wanted to make sure when I put it in bare a girl knows it's clean. 'Cause I ain't wearin' no overcoat.

— This is your life we're talking about and you just go for an AIDS test so you can stick it in bare?

— Yeah! You don't get that feeling with it on. You know when you wiggle and she can feel it. Telling you not to move out. You don't get that with a condom. But since you running scared you ain't gonna know.

— It ain't me that's having the AIDS test.

— Your next girl, give it to her without a condom and she'll tell you the difference.

— Yeah and you can get an AIDS test every time you get a new girl.

— Naw it ain't shit. Just a swab and piss into two jars.

— Swab?

— Yeah! They just push a cotton bud up your dick.

— Up your Jap's eye. Nah, I ain't havin' that.

— When it's been up there a while it . . .

— Fuck that. Ain't nobody puttin' nothing up my dick.

— No really, it ain't nothing. You don't feel a thing.

I feel sick already, go to cross my legs to keep my eyes from watering. I can already feel the intrusion of that cotton bud up my own dick. My imagination's always too vivid for my own good. I catch myself watching programmes and putting myself into the character's place and feeling their pain, their anguish. It just becomes a bit too much after a while and especially when it's my friend. I don't want to see him die, or even talking about his own mortality. Makes me question my own. Will I live to a ripe old age, have grandchildren, get married, all those socially acceptable things, or will I try it bare, get a girl pregnant and catch AIDS in the process?

— You're making me feel uncomfortable just thinking about it.

— But . . .

I cut Biggie short. I don't want him slipping into one of his monologues about the wonders of a full STD test. Trying to get everyone he knows to take one as well. Well, not this boy.

— No, just leave it. I ain't going for that.

— So who's the lucky girl that all this is for?

— What girl?

— Oh, so you doing all this just for your peace of mind?

— Yeah.

— Ah-huh.

— Why don't no one believe me? Q, you believe me?

— Eh! Leave me out of it. You lost me. Hey where's your bread?

— It's always for a girl. Remember Yasmina, you were gonna go Muslim for her. I still don't know how you got anything out of her. Rode all the way to Croydon for a piece of that pussy. Ethel in college, you got into photography for her.

— Eh, I ain't that bad. What about you and Jel-ica?

— What about us?

— Didn't see you for a good long time. Boning up on your philosophy!

— Just boning.

Q's snappy with the comeback and I can see him grinning from ear to ear. Happy.

— Shit, you two think you're comedians. Weren't me standing round with a branch stick-ing out of my knob.

— How many times I gotta tell you –

— No more times. You wanna be doing that then fine. But don't be coming and telling me about it like I want to know.

— Biggie. I found your bread but where's your jam?

— There ain't no jam, and don't bother going looking for no drink either, Mum ain't gone shop-ping.

— You mean you don't buy your own shopping?

Q's incredulous since his mum's been making him buy his own food since he started working and now that he's at uni he's still doing it.

— Fuck off, just 'cause you're a student now and scamming like a fucker.

— Scamming what? Free up with the freeness. The government ain't done shit for me so I'm out to get mine. The grant don't cover shit. Student loans, overdrafts, I'm in debt up to my eyeballs – of course I'm gonna get some money out of the government. You trying to say you ain't scamming?

— Sure I am, but I ain't using cash to buy food. I got garms to buy, records to purchase. Buying food – that's what mums are for.

— That's cold.

— Fuck you.

— No, fuck you.

— Fuck off.

— No, you fuckin' fuck off and flying fuck back to fuckin' Africa.

— You been saving that up for a long time.

— Yeah.

— Yeah what?

— What nothing.

I pause to catch my breath then look across at Q happily munching away on a jam sandwich. I'm always left wondering how he manages to reconcile the amount of food that he eats to his disciplined lifestyle policy. His mouth opens and in slides another huge chunk of food. He smiles at me and winks and I just break down into gales of laughter. Biggie looks at me as if I've suddenly grown horns, but I can't stop and for an instant I think my sides are going to split – but then I hold them together, arms wrapped tight around my sides, and the laughter starts to subside.

— What you bought lately?

— Nothing much, this and that.

— HMMMMMMMM!

— Don't be HMMMMing at my collection, just come out wid it.

— When did you get into Van Halen?

— Don't go getting all righteous on me, ain't me with the Led Zeppelin in my room.

— A person's gotta have range. Be able to like a lot of things.

— So what are you packing me into a tight box for?

— You ever been up a girl's virgin passage?

We both look at Q who has finished his sandwich and is sitting back looking at us.
— Yeah?

— What virgin passage?

— Her forbidden tunnel.

— You mean her dirtbox. No way, not me. Not this kid. I ain't going nowhere near that. I ain't going near no nasty crusty, bacteria-infested place when there's a lovely nice piece of muff just waiting for me.

— What brought this on?

— Just wondering.

I look at Q. He's into that evasive mode when he ducks questions by saying nothing's the matter and being all quiet and solemn, just letting the conversation take its course while he watches from the sides.

— It's Emily, isn't it? She's into anal sex.

Q stares at me hard and I see his eyes hardening as they pierce me. The old looks-could-kill slips to mind, but Biggie's already scenting blood and diving in.

— Emily, who's Emily?

— A girl. Listen, I just wanted to know whether you've ever done it, that's all. Nothing more, nothing less.

— Nah, there's got to be more otherwise you wouldn't have asked. You get all your info from books. You're looking for some advice. Here's some for free. Don't do it, son, you'll get shit clogged in your Jap's eye. It ain't worth it.

— Just leave it alone. When I'm ready to tell you I will.

— Just leave it, Biggie.

I butt in 'cause I know how Q feels – when someone's riding you hard, eager to get information out of you that you're not yet willing to give. And they don't care, they're just out to sate their desire for gossip, information that they can take and spread to as many willing listeners as possible. We all look around. It's uncomfortable, but we're friends, we'll get over it. It's just a matter of how long. You slip into zones in conversations when you just react and adapt to how other people are feeling and you move into a place where you become linked with them and their thoughts and feelings are mirrored by your own. That's how I feel now, my mood's locked into Q's, and I hate it when it happens – makes me too vulnerable – so I kick the conversation into another place, kick it out of its melancholic state back into territory that I'm familiar with.

— Me I just use old rubber johnny. He's my best friend.

— Sex without a condom, there is no finer act.

Biggie comes in with the info looking at Q as he does so. Then away, getting back into the swing of things.

— Pretend to put it on and then whip it in

bare, she'll notice the difference. I swear – AIDS test honour.

— Not me, I ain't getting no girl pregnant, I ain't ready for that sort of responsibility.

— Just say it weren't you. Deny everything.

— Am I the only 90s man here? In touch with my emotions, my feminine side.

— Fuck all o dat. Total and utter fuckrees. Give 'em a good seven inches, go muff diving a lot, lick her out, and they forget all that touchy-touchy, feely-feely bullshit.

— That's just cold blooded.

— It's what they want. Just give 'em what they want.

Radical shift of conversation direction initiated by myself.
— You got any blow?

— Nope. Free up with the freeness! Don't pay, won't pay. Why pay for something when I can get it free from someone else?

— Shit, we're gonna have to stop on the way to the Ministry so I can get some gear. I am definitely not going to the Ministry minus herb.

— You want to lay off that shit, it'll fuck you up.

Q's back in the game it seems, fresh and eager to run with the ball.
— Don't feed me that government propaganda, sensi is good all the way around. Anyway, don't knock what you haven't tried.

— I'd rather eat pork.

— Don't even think I'm going to go near that road.

— What road?

— Any road in which I gotta be in the front seat of a car driven by you, Q.

— Fuck off. You haven't even got a licence.

— What do you need a licence for? I know how to drive safely and under the speed limit. I ain't trying to be no fucking Nigel Mansell.

— I don't even drive and I agree with that.

— You don't know shit.

— You can't drive, Q, face it.

— Face what? I ain't sleeping with you.

— But you can't drive, Q. Really you cannot drive. I get scared being in the same car with you.

— What don't you like? Tell me, spell it out. Tell me why you think my driving is bad.

— You ride the kerb all the time.

— You go too fast.

— Drive too close to parked cars.

— You can't park for shit.

— You're always trying to knock down some pedestrian.

— Blatant use of the horn when it's not necessary.

Biggie pauses and I stop for a second to think

of some more allegations about Q's driving technique. This short pause turns into a gap into which Q can jump and give his defence, when what we want is to deny him space and just take him to the wall just like Daytona.

— For one, both of you don't drive. Two, you ain't got a licence so both of you ain't saying shit. All you're doing is pissing me off. I'm the one who drives both of you around town. I don't see you getting scared when I have to drive you off to Dalston or out to fucking Wembley. Both of you are fine then, aren't you? All the both of you do is bitch and moan. Well fuck both of you x amount of times sideways.

— Fornicate.

— What?

— Find another word. All you keep saying is fuck this, fuck that, fuckin' fuck fuck fuck. You're destroying my love of swearing.

— Listen to you Mr Swear-every-other-word-except-when-my-mother's-in-the-room. Read my lips: Fuck You.

— No. Fornicate you. There ain't that many swear words out there and to keep using the same ones is a denial of my verbal rights. You know when . . .

— No. Not another trip down memory lane.

— Cunt!

— Is it a bird? Is it a plane? No, it's another useless story from Meth.

— Anyway, a girl I knew, she thought she was a bit of an intellectual, she said to me . . .

— Get to it, get to it.

— Do you want to step outside?

— Only if it'll stop this story.

— She said to me that swearing was the sign of having a small vocabulary.

— Is that it?

— Thank you for that. Thank you. You have made my day.

— Makes me feel all warm and cuddly inside.

— Both of you. Bite the big one.

— What big one?

— Don't let me take it out.

— Listen to him, take IT out. Nothing there, mate.

— Bastard.

— Cunt.

— Wankmeister.

— Arselicker.

— Thank you, gratefully appreciated.

— Anytime, anytime.

— Met this girl.

— I knew it. Took a fucking AIDS test for a piece of puss.

— I met her as I was leaving, her name's Amanda.

— White or black?

— Does it matter?

— Sure bloody.

— Why? Why does it matter whether she's white or black? If I'm attracted to her that's all that matters.

— I've already had this conversation with him. He's set in his ignorant separatist ways.

— You as a black man should be going out with black women, not lusting after white flesh. I ain't into no bounties.

— Best keep that shit to yourself. You know how I feel about that.

— Well I ain't gonna be two faced and say one thing when you're there and another behind your back. You just wanna keep that jungle fever in check.

— What about Tanya? She was half-caste. You didn't have any qualms about dealing with her.

— She's light skinned, so what?

— Why do you have to keep going out with light skinned girls? I ain't seen you step to dark skinned girl once.

— What about Erika? She was as dark as me.

— So Erika was dark, that was an aberration. For as long as I've known you you've gone out with mixed race girls.

— You trying to say I wanna fuck white girls.

— Damn straight you do. You wanna fuck 'em but you go for light skinned girls cause you can't admit it. Me I'm honest. If I want a girl it don't matter whether she's white, black, Asian, Chinese or whatever.

— If being honest means fucking a white girl I'm gonna lie all my life.

Fight Gravity

*B*right lights, big city. London at night. Home of the brave, land of the free. They circle and wheel, spinning balls of light. Maelstrom of identity, slack and soft. Smooth and sweet. A city. The city. Never to disappear under the waves like Atlantis.

Huge shimmering waves of grey and white slanting hard across the night sky. Transmogrifying into a dark cover of shadow. A duvet of inkiness. An inkwell poured across the sky. Lights winking. Red and white, emanating, reflecting, twinkling. Starlike, going super nova. A ball of heat and light. Light, angel bright, angel strong. Energy flowing forth over the night shape. Batman's home. Dark, brooding, malevolent. A slanting leaning mass of concrete. Goliaths made of stone. Where is David to slay you? Slashing across the clouds, carving through them.

Killing them. Killing me. Killing you.

Light, life, hope. Under a blood red moon, oppressing powerful, a blood red moon for this heart that only makes war with thee. Crimson washing through me, mesmerising in its intensity. Fangs out, desire. Bare that throat to my *teeth, sup of that elixir of youth. Throbbing in the veins. The throat paper thin, translucent, supple and light. Never knowing, ceasing to care. Sky, stone, air. Elemental forces of nature. Never apart from, a part of. Nature entwined through you.*

Look up, see the clouds lit from beneath. Buildings just so many fingers pointing to the heavens. Stretching up, ever reaching. The heavens await. Ascension is upon us. Spiral upwards. DNA double helix, spiralling, turning. Compression of space, life. The city concrete heaven, glass hell. Driving, slanting, rushing claustrophobic centre of gravity. Can't get out. Always drawn back in.

No escape velocity. Ground zero, site of the blast. Event horizon spreading forever in every direction. Bending space, bending reality. But whose reality? Mine or yours? Individual states of being, expressions of reality. My reality: council estates, piss-filled lifts, youths roaming like packs of wolves, shape shifters, life on the edge. Dark, dangerous, erratic. Flickering lights, whispering voices, harsh sibilants, syllables rolling off the tongue, sliding along the ear, catching in the air. Rolling through the air like a loud noise in the storm of a headache, dreams that melt into nightmares that slide into waking moments. Lucid dreaming as the day slips by.

Look up, hear your name. Scream your name. Watch that clock tick away the time of your life. 12. Birth and death, hitting 4, young immortal, eternal. You can't kill me, you can't bend me. Defiant. Scream your name.

My reality, my reality. Grey, sombre, hard, sharp-

*edged. Unrelenting, unremitting. Never give up, never lie
down. Reality spinning away, shuttle launch. Light escap-
ing, no relating, no relation to life or time. Reality false
consciousness, false reality. Illusion. Nothing is real,
nothing to hold on to, reality slips away like tears in rain.
Like water through my fingers, running away. Mercury
rushing away, not light and insubstantial but heavy and
dense as lead. Thick and globulous, heavy and weighted.
My reality, your reality. Time moving backward from
death to birth.*

*Born to die. Born to fly. From pillar to post in an aqua-
marine world. Blue and green merging rainbow coloured,
shades of iridium swirling around. Do you know one
reality from another, can you tell the difference? Past
from present, future from past? Time, today, tomorrow.
Tonite, tonite. A night, the night. How many times in the
world's history has night escaped from its cage? Caged
and weighted down. The broken bars split at a molecular
level, split molecules flying apart. The bonds constraining
them ripped open. Night is abroad, running free, running
close and sharp to the breeze, keen razor slick.*

*Wrists held steady under the warm water as it pools
beneath. Swirling. Prick, pain, wrist action. Adapt, en-
dure, let the pain flow away. Slicing through, shooting up
to my heart. Thumping hard, move a mountain. Place
your hands against it. Feel it strong and sure. My heart,
the engine that drives me through this sea of iniquity.
Head going light. Fairies and sprites appearing at the
edge of my vision, dangling before my eyes. Gleaming*

diamonds, emeralds, amethysts, rubies, precious gems, precious life. Crimson crystallisation, pooling in the water, fairies transforming into sirens. Scarlet sirens calling me to a place where hope is denied and the night has no dominion. Dominion. Domination. Domesticity.

Deny it, deny the sirens, lost out. Sirens 2 Willpower 0. Lost out. Let the sun set no more, for I fear no man, woman or child. Deny my bestiality, clawing at my chest, trying to draw me back. Let it slide, let it all slide, and in the end, blood will out. Slip out like a limp penis. Desire sated. No more fighting, struggling.

My reality is this event. This period of time, this moment of sacrifice. Let my hands run red and my blood slip away into infinity. Infinity never knew my name and I curse her even as I yearn for her. Infinity squared, infinity denied. Denial of self, girl, duty. Loyalty. Honour. Tears in rain. I gave up fighting gravity long ago, when my reality caved into yours and all I could see was a wall all the way around. No way out, no way home. No hope of anything at all. Deny everything. Abandon hope, all ye who enter here, this maze of contrition. Absolutely not given. My reality has been twisted inside out and all I can do is watch and wait as my blood red self churns in front of me.

Speed Demons

— **H**ello! Yeah, can I speak to Jerome? ∴ .. Yeah, yeah, it's Meth. How you doing Liz? . . . Fine, fine. Still breathing. . . . Yeah I'm out of blow, yeah that's why I'm phoning. I'm going to this thing at the Ministry. . . . Yeah nuff man's on the guest list, can't be paying 20 shekels to get in.. . . Yeah you know that. Listen, tell him I want a quarter. . . . Yeah. I'll be there in a little while. . . . Where am I? I'm in a friend's car. . . . Yeah later.

Pull myself forward, turn off my phone and hang my head between the two front seats. Let it hang there.
— Take a left here.

The Cortina screams its pain as it heels over, tyres screeching, rubber left on the concrete. My face mashes against the door. I roll across the back seat, just another piece of flotsam in with

Q's mother's junk. Tissue boxes and covered cushions, travel blankets and crucifixes. Q's sitting in the front happy as a pig in shit, smiling, changing gear like a demon, the gear stick clutched loosely but surely in his fingers. Changing from 4th to 1st, his foot heavy on the brake – *Look ma, one hand!* – no stress on his face, just the tip of his tongue sticking out of his mouth. I feel like clicking my fingers behind my head, go on, work it boyfriend. But Q wouldn't appreciate it. So I scrunch lower and brace myself, trying not to look at the head rests, brightly coloured, rainbow coloured, Hawaiian-shirt-bright in their intensity. They glow eerily luminescent in the dark, catching the glow from the instruments and reflecting it back.

I hate driving in this car at night, everything about it conspires to make me feel uncomfortable. It feels as if ghosts are just lurking in the fabric of it, just waiting to spill forth and take over our bodies. Vessels for their nefarious designs.

I can feel my fingers itching. Want to feel that quarter in my hands, look at it, looking like old dried chocolate. That quarter is calling me, a haunting melody running through my brains and along my veins. I can smell that sweet smell now, achingly familiar in the intensity of feeling it pulls from me. Can feel the smoke sliding down my throat, feel the roach in my fingers held tight as I slip further into the fog, trying to pull the last effects from it.

— Left here.

Look out into the assault course. The adventure playground looming out of the darkness. Bright colours bright no more now – faded into an amorphous brown. The street lamps casting their orange glow far and wide. Beacons, sentinels, guardians of the night. They flicker on a level beyond human perceptions but I can feel them beaming their subliminal messages into my brain. Direct link into my cerebellum, up through my receptors, pushing through the gate into my frontal lobes.

— I know this place, the old dear's got a friend who lives round the corner. Used to bring me with her and I'd beg her to go and play on the adventure playground. She'd never let me though.

— Never?

— Nah, she'd keep me in, locked up in the flat with her friend's's daughter. Wasn't too bad.

— Just pull over here. Yeah, that's fine.

The door, the damn fucking door won't open.

I'm pulling at it like a mad man, cursing it, fighting it, foaming at the mouth. The shit door never opens from the inside. I'm winding down the window, spinning the winder in my palm, bicep bulging, forearm flexing. Pull it all the way down and pop the door open from the outside. Damn fucking child locks. I'm 21 years of age and I still can't decipher a child lock. Out the door and down the path before I remember and spin back.

— You coming?

Q pulls himself out slowly as if he's loath to come, while Biggie is all ready and willing to dive into the smoke-filled interior and get blunted. I chug up to the door and hug Liz as she steps out, swinging her around. Glad to see her, she's had her head shaved since the last time I saw her. Gone all Tank Girl, but without the little swirl of hair at the front. Bright eyes and a breathy voice all soft and whispery. A voice that conjures up images of sweat-stained sheets and passion sated for the moment. But she's not mine, not that any person's a possession, especially women. But I know I don't want to lose her as a friend. I'd love to lust after her and sometimes I slip into dog mode. Pinch my nose between thumb and forefinger and blow. Equalise the pressure, that feels better. Liz is away and through the door. Q and Biggie come up the steps, stopping at my shoulder, breath whispering against my ear.

— Who's she?

— Liz. Jerome's girl. Went to school with her.

— Honey and a half.

— Best believe it.

First impression of Jerome's den is of a huge space with a low fluffy ceiling. Lamps pushing out spinning coloured light onto the fabric-covered ceiling. Low fat cushions cover the floor with rugs covering the space that isn't covered by the cushions. Nothing is above head height, everything's low and squashed, candles are everywhere, supplementing the light of the coloured lamps. The candlelight flickers as a soft breeze drifts through the room. It took Jerome ages to find a parachute for his ceiling. He's lying on the floor – where else could he lie? He doesn't have a bed – across four cushions, neck bent at an impossible angle, arms spread crucifixionlike, mouth open catching flies. A strange warbling like birds in the morning echoes around his head.

Liz drops down over by the system and tweaks the volume up a bit and Anita Baker's soaring vocals swell and roll around the room, rushing from the speakers hidden behind the canopy, making the erotic eastern sexual positions painted onto the walls as huge murals come alive with passion. They seem to dance in front of my eyes, as if only by the activation of Anita's voice can they come to life.

I kick Jerome's bare foot and watch him jerk awake, a slow grin spreading across his face. Jerome's all elastic and dipped in honey. Sticky and slow. Not lethargic, just mellow. As if he could move fast if he wanted to but he just doesn't want to. He's got a delicate air about him that makes his movement slow and gentle as if he's engaged in a constant bout of tai chi. His eyes glow with recognition and his whole face lights up.

— Meth!

He stretches wide, white teeth, glowing softly. Bull ring swinging in a slow mesmerising arc – back and forth, back and forth – as he rolls forward into the lotus position. Pulls his scales out of a mass of cushions, dull brass gleaming, rubbed soft and hazy. He starts measuring as I flop forward.

— Jerome, I'd like you to meet my friends Q and Biggie.

— Hey, nice to meet you, guys.

— How's things, Jerome?

— Good good. My sister, she's coming back from Amsterdam tomorrow.

— How's her café going?

— Good, good. You know Paulette, everything she puts her mind to she does well at. Me I just take things easy.

— True, true.

He's measuring out my quarter, moving the little weights back and forth with the mounds of herb resting in plastic bags, a little Haagen Dazs taster spoon moving quantities between bags. I'm watching, mesmerised, until I drag my eyes away and look for the board, lifting it out from under my butt. My face is level with the dressing table covered with candles, the accumulated wax making a wave, dripping down the sides, frozen and still. Scoot around so I can free the jack knife from my back pocket and open it with a flick of my wrist. Hear its oiled click as it locks. Jerome hands over the bag and I spill it on to the board and proceed to chop, doing my best chef's impression, fingers over the blade as I dice my herb into ever smaller chunks. Retreating into a tunnel with only chopping at the end of it. When I sit back and slide the contents of my board into a bag, Jerome's got this spliff burning and hanging Hilda Ogden-style from his lower lip. Inhales deep, blowing out a shifting plume of smoke, a writhing dragon. Leans forward and hands it to me, a grin splitting his face.

— Try before you buy.

I grin back and take it, put it to my lips and inhale quickly, taking it down smooth and slow, nice and easy, feel it run across my chest. Hold it there and then push it out in one long breath. Head goes light, eyes feel heavy. He must have made it out of pure grass. My eyes feel red already. I'm pulling on it again, blowing my head off in a mellow explosion of sensation. I hand it to Biggie slightly bereft already, but joyous inside. Reach into my pocket and start digging out my cash. Rumpled notes spread out in front of me as I take a very long time peering very closely at them to see which ones are which. Pick out a twenty and a fiver, lay them flat and try to unwrinkle them. I do have some pride.

— 25 big ones.

— For you, Meth, 15.

— No. Jerome, take my money.

— No. 15 and nothing more.

— Liz isn't pregnant, is she?

I turn to her and shout-whisper.
— You're not pregnant, are you, Liz?

She laughs that soft laugh she has, hides her mouth behind her hand and shakes her head as the laughter takes over her.
— If she's not pregnant why you being so generous?

— Because I can and my sister's bringing me over a very big plant tomorrow, so I'm not worried about losing out on a tenner.

— OK. Who am I to argue with my dealer? 15.

I hand over the cash and stagger to my feet, giving Jerome a big hug before following Liz out, giving her another hug at the doorway and feel the cold breeze rip into me, trying to pull my stoned feeling away from me. Trip down the steps checking my pockets to see if the gear's still there. It is. Pull open the door and flop onto the seat to wait for Q to start driving.

The Burial

Q pulls away from the kerb and down the lit street, charging up to 90 in a 30 mph zone. I'm stoned in the back with my chin stuck to my chest and I'm ready to go. I just need something to jump-start my energy level. I lean forward, stretching, reaching, fingers clawing at the air as I try desperately to turn on the radio. I'm a fake ass wrestler trying to make a tag, having been beaten on for the past ten minutes, as I stretch closer and closer, with my opponent close, breathing down my neck. Find a massive spurt of energy and dive forward into the tag. I hit the knob with my forefinger and spin it on. The car jumps a beat as the music comes in. I fall back, released. Slumped in the back, eyes half closed, head nodding on the beat. Dance to the bass, close my eyes and slip away.

A crystallisation of thought and sound. Crystal

forming, pressurised, crushed flat. Broken. Pressure exerted, new forms created, faceted mirrorlike. Reflection of reflection of reflection. Eyes caught, iris wide, attraction, sensation, rub along the palm, brush light, gasp. Dry throat from a sunbeam to a sunray. Flooding illuminating. Wind, wave, colliding, collapsing. Breaking down. Watch it roll, high peak. Flowing trickle like water.

53 inches above sea level, 93 million miles above these devils. soaring, punching through the atmosphere into the clear inky jetness of space. Tumble frozen. A statue in motion. Contradiction of self and space. No weight, but momentum carrying me forward. Vacuum. No sound, purgatory. Median. Space between.

Fall backward. Heat, force, tumble. Fall, fall. Icarus. Clipped wings, flight curtailed. Flesh burning, searing, scorching. Ripped from me in strips, flowing behind me. My cloak, my form. Fall forever and ever and ever and ever and ever. Eternity waiting below me. Eternity covering me.

Slip through time – past, present, future.

Whose future? Images within my skin curling forward, wrapping around me. Images, my skin tattooed with light, with form. Fall, fall. Lights around me, angels calling.

Eyes open and I hear the call for the rewind. Strange nebulous underwater sound as the DJ spins that record backwards. Q's already leaning forward to boost the volume to try and blow his mum's speakers. I sink back even further into my seat and let Leviticus flow over me. The Burial. Those angel voices whisper and hum. The sound soft and gentle. OOOOOOOO! Hearing it my spine tingles: I know what comes next. Breath comes quicker, head nodding with the bassline that hasn't arrived yet. An imperceptible move-ment. Neck driven, wind assisted. A leaf moving in the breeze. Let the intro go. Hear it for what it is. An intro. A space before the bass, a signature, maker's mark. Letting you know what's coming next and who's coming next. So we sit and wait, letting it come towards us from the depths of subliminal bass. To heart, overtaking strident patterns of aural imagination. The Burial. As the bass makes itself know Shaquille O'Neal style, slamming its way through the speakers, heads move forward in unison, nodding. Getting it. The knowledge that you dance on the bassline, not the beat. The bassline. Bass it all. Going back to the beginning of everything. Our primal tribal roots. Our African ancestry. The tribal notes, the lost civilisation of drum and bass. What makes black music so special is the bass line. Bass that overrides the heartbeat, that interrupts its normal pattern, its normal rhythm, and makes it move to the bassline. Bass is the vanishing point on the horizon where all black music disappears back to. The rhythm that heartbeat which entwines itself around your own, pulsing with it. Taking it to another dimension.

Heartbeats thumping strong and powerful.

Bass. The beginning and the end. The rhyme with no omega. Clip your wings and bring you down to earth an show you what life is worth.

Bass. The heartbeat. The bassline becomes you on a level that is impossible to define, so close are you. Drum and bass the engine that drives Jungle. It drives us as we nod our heads to *The Burial*.

Before *The Burial*, there was *The Helicopter Tune*, *Shuffle*, *Sweet Love*.

After *The Burial* there is *Warning*, *Dead Dread*, *Fire* and they keep coming.

Anthems for a generation returning to its spiritual home. I let it all wash over me, leaving me limp. Head nodding. Jungle is me and I am the Jungle – no distinction, no separation. Siamese twins joined at the chest, the heart. Try to pull us apart and we die. Can't and won't live without you.

I pull out my phone and turn it on, pushing the address button, scrolling through until I get to the right number, push dial and wait. Connection.

— Yeah I'd like a big shout out to . . .

Guestlist

Mr Meth

The guestlist is a strange and curious thing. A way of getting into club nights for free, but like everything else in life it has a pose value. A very high one at that. Being on the list shows you've got clout, that you know somebody, somewhere. That you are part of the elite who make the money rather than parting with it. The easier you are admitted the more status you possess. If like us you have to wait and queue up like the other plebs on the guestlist, rather than being sped through, you know how far you still have to go up the status ladder. Most are just glad to not be paying huge amounts of money to be getting into a dance. Even though you're on the guestlist still don't make you immune from the search: supposedly for your own safety and to keep the club a drugs free zone. Some places aren't too bad, others are just out to make you feel small and they might as well be concentration camps. Me I put my gear and my papers in my sock. If you're wearing ankle-high boots you're free and clear. Carry my cigs in their box, just make sure there aren't any half-used ones still in there and you're away.

I hate queuing. It's one of the reasons I started getting on the list, so I wouldn't have to queue, but I find I spend more time queuing than if I'd bought a ticket. But what I hate more than queuing is paying to get in somewhere. After a few times of freeing up with the freeness, I've found that I now become distinctly aggrieved whenever coughing up cash to go somewhere comes up. So in the end my miserliness overrules my hatred of queuing as I'd rather queue and get in free than spend money and get in immediately.

Walk around the corner and find the queues 10 across and 30 deep. Over the other side there's a queue just as large which seems to be moving a hell of a lot faster. Bowl up to the security guard and try to confirm my suspicions. Look up and down the line for anyone I know. If there is, do a bit of a bounce, jump in with some old friends. We just get the stares, people sizing you up. Male and female. Faces turned away in conversation, whispering into someone's ear. A gale of laughter rolling down the line. Shoulders hunched against the wind. Breath white on the wind. Hands shoved deep into pockets, feet stamping. The general air of people being treated like cattle. Made to wait and wait and wait. Stand and watch others ushered in.

Get to the security guard standing there in his black bomber jacket with the name of some security firm emblazoned on it. Standing behind those metal security barriers the police always bring out at Trafalgar Square on New Year's. Touch his shoulder to get his attention. He's big – they generally are, I think it's part of the job description. His neck's thick and wide from pumping those weights. His muscles hidden but the bulk they have created not. His crew cut hard and savage. He turns slowly and looks us up and down. Slow and easy.

— Where's the queue for the guestlist?

He points back at the queue we've just passed and I'm already pissed off. I hate walking down a queue expecting to get in and when you get turfed having to make your way back down that same queue. Looking in those faces and having to either slink away or take you station at the end. We walk back and I look over at the queue for the ticket-holders, a surging mass of people being let in in groups of 30 at a time, almost tripping over themselves to get inside.

Push and shove, doing everything except sprinting to get ahead of their neighbours. I follow Q and Biggie, meeting any eyes looking at me, not showing any shame. Can't let 'em see me get down. Fuckin' guestlist. Times like these I don't know whether to laugh or cry. You want to be inside so badly you can smell the condensation on the walls already.

The muffled sound coming from inside. A bass so heavy you can still feel it through the building walls. Making you want to dance in the line. Whenever you hear a tune you love, it burns in your chest that you can't be inside listening to it properly. The line moves forwards a few steps here, a few steps there. People join at the front, walk down the queue and jump into it seeing a friend or two. We just wait – Q and Biggie engaged in a conversation in quiet tones while I lean back and listen to the voices around me.

— You should have seen her, she was gonna kill him.

— Nah it ain't all that. You want to play Killer Instinct. Game and a half.

— Never wanted to be anything else.

— Damn it's cold.

— I'm at college now, I want to do a degree next year.

— What time is it?

— Can I ponce a cigarette? Cheers.

— Got a light? Thanx.

— I seen better-looking girls.

— What do you mean? If Arsenal didn't have Ian Wright they would have been relegated long ago.

The conversations take on a meaning all of their own, creating a patchwork of overlapping lives, events, thoughts and motivations. Everyone a microcosm of reality. A different slant on it, a different take. But everyone comes together at this one point and it feels as this one point is where they were always bound. That from the moment the sperm hit the egg they were destined to come here to have their conversations, to spill forth their appointed lines and become part of my reality. Ripples in my pond.

The Ministry

The Ministry, the ultimate in sound reproduction. Bass so clear, full and deep, it makes you feel like weeping at the sound of it. Like an angelic chorus. Bass driving deep into the fibre of my being. There's something just so wonderful about the main room pumping out Jungle while the bar area and chillout room are playing House and Garage. It constantly brings a smile to my face. I look up from the contemplation of my boot into Q's eyes; gleaming at the prospect of a night of Jungle. How his body is restless and impatient to be inside the box, wanting to be in there dancing. Letting the beat get inside you and take you away into the zone, where your eyes close and you're aware of nothing but the bass. The music and you are one.

One life, one bass and one destiny. I order you to dance for me. I put my hand on his shoulder and feel the energy running in him like he's on speed.

— Calm down, I wanna put my jacket in the cloakroom.

I have to shout to make myself heard over the music. We're standing just in the entrance to the box and as we move back through the bar area we've already lost Biggie. We're not likely to see him for the next 6 hours. Chuck my coat in the cloakroom, letting my eyes roam. Lots of people just standing up drinking. This is where you make eye contact: you see them, they see you and you move towards each other as if an invisible cord binds you. Complete load of bollocks, but some people believe it. At this moment in time I'm not interested, I want to jump up.

I step into the box, following Q's square back, the flashing lights reaching out like searchlights, pinpointing me, like tracer streaming through the air, arcing over me and the packed dancefloor. Squeeze through the sweating heaving bodies, whistles being blown constantly, the string wet with sweat. Foghorns held in loose hands, slapping against thighs. Inch our way through, looking for a pocket of space.

Don't want to be stuck against a wall, want to be in the thick of things, creating space with your elbows, getting into the zone. The bass is overwhelming, created on planes and levels of which

I hadn't even conceived. Planes of aural sensation, overlapping subliminal bass, thumping into my chest. Freight weight bass rolling over me. The rumblism in full effect. Rolling bass that powers over you, assaults the senses in its intensity, rollin' like thunder. From back to front a wave of sound, heartbeat-stopping rumblism.

An avalanche of sound, pushing the edge of the aural envelope, not to be denied. But above it scalpel-sharp, thin layers of treble, running high and pure. No distortion at all. Presence, soundstage. Bass and treble in complete harmony. High note heaven.

Slip into overdrive. Put my head down and run. Run on the spot, arms driving loose and limp. Take me up and never let me go. Take me up into the stratosphere on angel wings. Up to the moon, pitted face, craters and the sea of tranquillity. Flashing lights moving behind my closed lids, explosions of rainbow colour as I sway and shuffle my feet.

Not yet lifting them high. Sliding into it, soft and easy. I just want to let it all go. Let myself disappear into the abyss of sound before me, fall into it never to return. Layers of blue darkness, reaching a depth of intensity that tears the nerves apart then splices them back together with a new gene inserted. I'm falling even deeper into a substance over which I have no control. A substance that rolls forward, taking over me. My destiny is entwined with it. Its ups and downs are my ups and downs. I dance and sway, shuffle my feet and sing along, shouting myself hoarse. The music entering my blood. I dream that it's spilled out thick and red, running free.

Nothing to do but to lose myself, slip in and out of it. The bass rides hard on my heart, guiding me down the paths of aural intoxication. Lost in the woods of sound. Bass all around me changing shape and form. Fairies trapped for millennia within the bass. Old as time, they awaken and dance across my eyes, at the edge of my vision. Moving as if blown by the wind. I pull out my lighter and flick it, revealing dark shapes to be people, young people, fresh and free, not worn down by life or weighted down with the unbearable bleakness of being. Not questioning their own mortality or station in the world. What am I here for? What does it all mean? Bullshit meaningless mumblings of a generation ahead, which we will fall into eventually, but right now we have enough energy to create our own path before we become locked to the ones already made.

Flashing my lighter I look around, move across the crowded space, peering into faces. Light sparking, eyes illuminated as heads turn and stare. I grin and move on, let 'em see the whites of my teeth. See her all around, smell of her flower fragrance, sharp, pungent. Powerful, musk-like in its intensity, in its ability to overwhelm the senses, capture them. Tie them to its own covert purposes. Sliding across the nostrils seconds after she'd passed. Déjà vu, reminiscence. Bodies together, her scent on me, my scent on her. Sweat subdued underneath the perfume. Flower scent rolling strong. Attraction smell, forest fire, jungle desire. Burning within me as I watch the girls dance.

Heartbeat racing, accelerating, lifting into high gear. Sweat coming off the body, dripping down the walls. Steam in the air. The girls dance eyes closed, uninterested in you looking at them. Tight hot pants, exposing buttocks you've dreamt about lying on. Legs encased in stockings that end at mid thigh, knee-length boots with a tower block of hooks for the long lace to weave round, overlaying tight calves. Thighs spasming, muscles clenching and contracting. Long legs taut and cut. An agony of looking, wanting.

Breasts encased in lycra, nipples erect pushing through the fabric, demanding to be noticed. Belly button exposed on a plain of flatness. Muscles moving beneath the skin, hard and to die for. Tongue running along it. Hair flicked from their faces as their arms create abstract shapes only they know exist. They are in the zone. Cut off from us mere mortals who still exist on just one plane of creation. They have been transported to that sphere where thoughts are bound to the music and the bassline is your heartbeat. You become the music and the body you exist in becomes a vessel to be filled by it. So they dance, legs pistoning, feet sliding over the floor, bare legs caressed by the wind. Long trails of sweat rolling down to the ankle where a gold chain leaps a little every time they move. Exposed to the carnivorous gaze, hips swinging, legs locked and straining as they stand their feet apart, shaking that booty. Buttocks weaving in a circular motion, hands on their thighs, bent over ready to be entered, inviting, rotating, one foot lifted, shaking their stomachs, making their butts shake and shiver, ripples of motion sliding beneath the fabric that encases them.

They dance, dervishes in motion. My heart burns for them. Tight lithe forms, how I burn for you. Like a moth to the flame, my eyes return to watch you dance. Shake that thang. Got to have you, possess you. Make you mine. Make you all mine. I'm a 90s man. In touch with my feelings, maybe. So I watch, my lust in check as I peer at you through the darkness. Occasionally you are silhouetted and I see you truly. I'm here to enjoy

myself, enjoy the music – to sweat, to dance in
an aural maze letting the basslike clouds roll
overhead. Ever advancing, moving inexorably
forward. No stopping them. Two states of being.
Watch that bottom writhe within those golden
hot pants. How I love them. Hot pants showing
what you've got.

Strong yet fragile at the same time. Duality of
nature, being able to have enough confidence to
expose yourself to the hungry gaze, but also for
it to be there to be attacked at any time and
fearful of this happening. Wearing your heart out
there on your sleeve, out there for all to see.
These girls excite me, entice me, fascinate me,
seduce me. The way they dance, the way they
move. How they present themselves, aggressive,
going out for self and the devil take the hind-
most. Able to revel in their own femininity, their
own sexuality, making of it a strength rather than
a weakness. As the darkness envelopes them
they dance on, asking for the stares, courting
them, desiring them, then denying the emotion
it engenders. They have made this their playground and you enter it knowing the rules: they
can say no at any time and the game stops there.
No replays, no extra time, no penalty shoot out.

I leave the box and hit the world outside. Grab
a drink and am surprised as always by the ex-
tortionate amount of money it costs. You'd think

they imported Snapple from the sun at these prices. At least I know that they don't turn off the tap water in the toilets as they do in some places. Lean on the bar and look out, while the house DUFFs behind me. A nice crowd: all nations, all creeds represented. The uniforms in effect, names roll thick and fast, heavy with dollar importance: Ralph Lauren (old Ralphie), Armani, Yves St Laurent, Moschino, Versace, Stone Island, Schott, Timberland, Karl Kani – all of the commanding big bucks. Fashion commandeered by those who don't have any money but find ways of gaining access to it to keep up with the roller coaster that is style.

Fashion out there on the edge of credibility, watch it teeter as it is rebuilt and re-formed by those who *live* the life that fashion so desperately wants to portray, who take what is given and warp it into something else entirely. And then fashion, that huge industrial complex, swings into action and quickly grabs it, bastardises it and sells it back. Saturates the market. By which time those who created the style have long since moved on, the perpetuating loop rolling on down the block.

I'm out of the loop 'cause I don't have enough dollars to afford them steep prices, and the little jobs I do now and again aren't enough to cover a major clothes habit. So I save myself the trouble and don't start down that road.

Head back to the box, a Snapple in my hand, to immerse myself in the healing sounds. Deep and dark. Step in and I am immediately swallowed by sound. Slipping away into nothingness.

Three the Hard Way

We were dead from morning and now shit ain't changed. In this Jungle we were Nature's strongest breed looking down upon our Reeboks and didn't survive the battle, our hearts just took the pain.

— High on stress ... babae ... We live in Brixton babae.

— He's singing again.

Only we take from life, in exact amounts, what we put in. Down past the offie, across the tags, past Paul's barber shop packed with heads, nuff buds a roast in the air, the jeweller's shop, the butcher's (Halal) we move.

— We live in Brixton ... babae.

— What the fuck are you singing?

— We live in Brixton ... *babae.*

Three The Hard Way. When the shit gets too thick in this surround, we burn and get high on stress: We run tings they say tings ne run we. There's a dirty stain in the air but we don't care cause home's only moments away and war is life in the everyday.

— We live in Brixton ... *high on stress ... babae.*

Only on this part of the earth, crime pays, so when crime doesn't pay, you know it had to be free. In this business they are the empire. If they ever meet God He'll understand. In the chillout room the phones sings, the tones of niggas hustling ends. Ain't shit moves unless we on it or fucking it. Everyday's a fight, a fight from falling from gravity's pull into the Earth.

— Yeah? ... What, What? ... What? Slow down! ... Who? ... Did what? ... Craig? ... Craig!

Craig's Prayer

I WANT TO LEAVE THIS PLANET FROM ALL THE TROUBLES THAT'S IN IT.

Lately I've been thinking, maybe I'm sick, I should see my doctor but still it don't matter. Sitting on the edge of my bed, stressed in my four cornered room with thoughts that go nowhere, come back, disappear. Maybe God's fucking with me. This shit just dogging me.

I inhale then exhale as night creeps into day, as the dawn brings the beginnings of another dark Saturday morning. In go the freaks of the night and out come the good Christian folk of the city. In this bonded state I just stare and stare, people passing through the waking streets, conversing, listening to the voices of the peoples, since in this the world knowledge and ignorance are both on offer and I only listen, digest, consider – and we'll just say it's shit. In the dawn of this day I feel fear closing in. I want a place where I can go to be mad.

I remember castles in the sand, and once I stopped looking they'd disappear, die. Ashes to ashes, dust to dust. Fuck I just don't know. Do ants ever stop and question what goes on? In this rat race, you look up, get concerned while others pass on by and check it, see who comes to your side. Friend or foe? – What's goin' on? Listen ... The ghettoised state of mind speaks with blacken statements scrawled on a white wall. Peripheral noises rising from the ghettos are the whispers which turn to screams when comes time to change. Gods into dogs and dogs with human heads, dogs chewing bones off the master's table. Life is now born from concrete cracks and fed on the barrel of a gun, while thought is the trigger, firing lead into the mind, causing momentary spasms of life, real life; this is the people, these are the peoples. Migrants from gracious lands, coming into the cold and sometimes – just sometimes – this grace is released, love speaks: broken chains lie helpless without the power of the master and the ghost from our gracious lands speak. One day I might speak with love, with form, perception, wisdom, where my words are brighter than the sun and live and create their own light. Coking up my life. This, the land of the blind, the one-eyed man is king. Nothing surprises those who see as the world rises with the sun. Everything that exists will be illuminated and I will stay in the shadows by myself for myself, for each and every day. Each passing season will bring life closer and further away. The pain will maintain, 'cause it runs deep into the hearts of the brave and strong. This is the war in Babylon.

Only Mum could come and take away the ghosts so that I can live and maintain. If only this can of T wouldn't run out, if only . . .

Saturday
Da Flipside

"Death to the young is the undiscovered country"
MAYA ANGELOU

Everyman

Another grey day comes from another grey night, shutters go up on the shop front windows, signs and graphics are like beacons showing the way. If the price is right and your pockets have change, pay. As the harmonies of voices rise into the air, people seep out from the street corners. When *tings a gwon*, it's real. The TV will only give you cartoon reflections of these streets. Being born of flesh and brought up on concrete gives your mind, body and soul a whole new function for living.

There are some things you'll never know, least of all understand, even if it's just your rights. How many youts who shift through the streets are made to realise that they have a mind that can cure cancer? You will never know that you'll inherit the earth because you'll never be told. How many times have you got to have your head banged against a wall before you realise the pain, before you realise the pain this world brings is man made and your head's against the wall every day? One day you'll know what this life owes you. The question shall always remain, how many rivers do we have to cross before we realise we've lost and the yout turns back and steps out on the streets. This way of life is love and loved in the jungle.

Craig looked back as a child, when he would be dragged through the streets, through the markets — first Bush, then Bricky, later Peckham — and hear the riddim of Reggae, looking at the skirts of aunts, playing on the streets with his cousins, running with the wind in his shaven head looking out into tomorrow.

Craig came up the hard way. His mother was like a black monolith, his father only existed as a ghost in his past. She never let Craig forget he was her firstborn and her last, she would never allow him to forget the pain. His life is an extension of hers and as such, with the skin he's in, his world would never be sweet and he always remembered someday would come the payback. The pain, the love, the joy and the reward, with all the stories she told of her struggle to succeed, a struggle she had fought for him — he would always believe his struggle would finish it. The truth is it never would.

Every Saturday he made his trek across London to visit his babymother. Today, as the

time came to 11 o'clock he was late with a hang-
over that cast a deep shadow on his mood: it
seemed he was driven there more by obligation
than by love. The journey took him up the
Victoria Line to Oxford Circus, Central Line
towards East Acton and a short walk to Du Cane
Road.

> Craig Mac! 1000 *degrees*
> You'll *be* on *your knees,*
> You'll *be*
> *Burn begging please.*
> *I'm a reign, reign forever,*
> *Rain like bad weather.*

It's always a Saturday when Craig imagines a
verse and sings, when he regroups, creates a verbal technique, a kung fu from the mind
re-enacted over and over, re-enacted into
various riddims, finally resting in a Reggae ska.

His yout was called Tony. He would have gone
as far as calling him Tony Montana but no one
would have understood, that is, how he always
wanted to be a gangster. A gangster that would
chat like an armed soldier of Jah, schooling them
on certain runnins. All this, like most thoughts,
was just passing in the wind. Only in the eyes of
Craig's son would this vision be true, only Tony
would listen intently – as children do sometimes, picking on dreams.

Natasha watched over them while they

played, eyeing him all the time: his new clothes, his new haircut, his new shoes. Craig always made a point of looking good and Natasha always took this as a sign he had money. Thus she'd begin, pulling her usual yam:

— Doing well, are ya?

— What you chatting about?

— I'm talking about money to feed your yout.

That made him sore. She would always hassle him for money, never once standing on her own two feet, never looking to do for herself. It was always Craig, *what have you done for me lately*? It didn't bother him paying for Tony's keep but it seemed he was paying for her indulgences.

— You lazy bitch, you're so fucking lazy! Why the fuck don't you go out and work?

No reply.
— That's cool, because now I'm going to make you work.

With that he puts Tony in his room, pulls Natasha to the bedroom, tying her up with her clothes, and goes for his belt. He goes out and grabs all her perfumes and sprays and systematically beats the shit out of her, pulling off her clothes just to beat the raw skin. He stops, picks up the perfumes and sprays, pouring them into her raw wounds.

— Fuck you, bitch.

And so saying, he makes her bend over and spread her legs apart.

— Now, here's your shit.

And taking fifty pounds out of his pocket he crumples it and shoves it up her crutch.

Mr Meth: Exit Stage Left

I stagger out into the morning air, crisp and cold, breath frosting on the breeze. Looks like I'm smoking. How often as a kid did I stand around outside pretending to smoke in the cold air. Shiver for a second as I stamp my feet and pull on my jacket, retrieved from the wilds of the cloakroom. Quick look at my watch. Half 4. Watch the seconds hand flick round, mesmerised by its circular movement. Life is like a circle, wheels within wheels, turning, turning. Another quick tug at the jacket, pulling it up to my throat and sliding the zip closed.

Turn around and look back, feeling the people brush past me – a rock in the sea of their movement. You know it's a good night when people are still trying to get in to a club when you're leaving. They are still standing and waiting, watching you as you leave – looking to see how you feel as you walk past, as if by your expression and demeanour they can fathom out whether it is worth going in, paying those extra dollars on the door. Their hard eyes gleam like cat's-eyes in the road, reflecting light back at you, watching as you stand and try to not look conspicuous. When you're standing in line looking at people is the most interesting thing you can do.

Watching them watching me, caught in the cross hairs of a sniper's scope, dead to rights; laser light on my forehead, finger around the trigger. Spill my brains over the pavement. Crowd round like the voyeuristic vampires that you are and stare. Lifeless, my bodies lie there becoming colder, more rigid, more adult, whilst I stare into your eyes and see you yearn to see a spectacle. To see someone die in a particularly gruesome Quentin Tarantino fashion. Your faces are cold and hard, eyes sharp as flint, bodies lean like greyhounds waiting to be unleashed.

Turn my head away from your gaze and look behind me. See Biggie and Q saying their good-byes. Fists touching, complex handshakes given and finished with a flourish. Watch them smile and nod gently. Tired but pleased. Happy to have gone but ready now to go home to settle comfortably into their own homes, familiarity all around them. Didn't get any puss but not exactly trying very hard.

They walk over to me and I see them slip into slow motion, each footfall arriving long seconds after it was taken. Gentle loping stride, as they are floating, each detail of them etched into my memory as they tussle gently and then look over at me: eye contact, acknowledgement. I feel a huge flush of emotion slide over me, a comfort in the knowledge that they are here with me. Q all rolling gait, wide and broad as if he is striding across the deck of a ship at sea, arms close to his body as he listens to Biggie expounding on some subject. His face set into a mask of concentration, intent to listen to every word and understand it. Biggie with his small frame and sweeping movements, hands creating intricate patterns, feet spread outward duck-fashion. Walk bouncy and slightly pimp limpish, rising on the balls of his foot every step. I blink and everything comes back up to speed and I stand here trying to act nonchalant and devil-may-care, seemingly unaware of the passing glances. Wondering whether my fly is undone, trying not to check. They reach me and I feel so close to them that it hurts, so close that I treat them like family. Hurt them unintentionally but accept and trust that they'll be there when I regain my senses. That they will always be there to support me and keep me going when times are rough.

Zip up my emotion-proof jacket and pull the soft vulnerable parts of myself back into my shell. Cassie showed me how vulnerable I was when I thought that I was indestructible. She slipped in under my guard and loved me and I loved her just as I love these guys. I thought I had everything locked up in the box, but it popped open and I couldn't get the lid back on. All the emotion I'd held inside just spilled out and I couldn't put it back on as long as I was with her. So I left.

You can't be soft with life. Any show of weakness and the sharks appear, ready to feast on you – scenting blood, moving in silent and deadly, tearing strips out of you, driven into a frenzy of feeding. Open the box within yourself where all the secret parts of you are kept, lift the lid and find that all the privileged information it contained comes back to haunt you. Spat out in the heat of the moment, faces touching, voices loud and harsh as the anger spits forth like venom. Searing the skin, burning through the layers, burrowing through to the bone. Bone showing pearly white in its luminescence, gleaming as clear as day. So I hide myself beneath layers of toughened skin. Skin toughened through a youth as normal or abnormal as anyone else's. Just as the gradual accumulation of scars through a life of rough and tumble, wear and tear of being human and as fragile or strong as anyone else, and as unable to change your lot as anyone else. A lot that is dominated by skin colour. Whether brown, black, white, yellow, there is no getting away from it. Chocolate brown complexion that evokes such fear and loathing, but also suppressed desire. Lusted after yet also despised. Second class citizen. So you hold everything inside, not going to let it ever get out. Hold it all in. Death grip, grip so tight my knuckles go white. Got to break the fingers to loosen it.

My friends trip the light fantastic as they step to me and nudge me back into intelligible thought. Wrap my arms around them and hug them, my friends. Try not to smile, to laugh, to give an indication that just being with them makes me about a foot taller. Walking on a buoyant cushion of air. Walking tall in their company.

— Where'd you go? I lost you. One minute you were there, the next you were gone.

— You know me: Undercover Elephant. Now you see me, now you don't.

— What are we doing now?

— Going back to the car, that's what we're doing.

— No after-dance parties?

— Get to the car first then we'll decide.

The windscreen of the Cortina is covered in huge glossy fold-out, gatefold, expanding-to-twice-their-size-if-immersed-in-water flyers. Bright colours streaking through the air. A new dawn on Q's windscreen. We rip them from underneath the wipes and bundle inside, turning up the radio and the heating, pouring through them, seeing where they are, watching the lines of force as Jungle travels up the country, trying to figure out where it's going to blow up next. Birmingham, Northampton, Luton, Manchester, Leeds. Seeing how long it takes and how far it goes. After sifting through them, amazed at the size and colour, bitching at the prices and deciding that we can't be bothered travelling into the wilds of the northern hemisphere, the flyers are chucked onto the floor and disregarded until Q has to clean it out before his mother drives it again.

— So where we going now?

Loud and brash. *Top of the world, ma. Top of the world*.

— Home.

— Nah! There must be a party somewhere. I feel to go somewhere, do something.

— Well I feel to go home and sleep in my own bed.

— Come on, the night's young.

— I'm with Meth. It's only half 4. I feel to keep going.

— You know we're going to crash at someone's and I always hate that.

— Live a little.

Q looks at me as if I've lost the little sense in my head. Cut him some slack though, because he does have a hard time sleeping in other people's houses. It comes from not settling down for a long time, so he likes to know that he's in his own house, which is permanent; that's what he said a few months back. I ruffle his semi afro and smile a goofy grin into his face. Don't you just love me? He looks at me for a long beat, quizzical, wondering. Then he shakes his head and leans down to put the key into the ignition. I jump up and down on the back seat like a kid who's just been told he will be having ice cream and not later but right this minute.

And like Fame I'ma live forever,
Niggas crossing over 'cause they don't know no better.

Q straps himself in and pulls out intent on breaking the land speed record, revving the engine like he's out of control, but the grin he flashes to Biggie is self-deprecating: in this instance, for this short space of time, he knows what he's doing, he's just pissing about, having a little fun. Joking at his own style of driving.

— Head for Camden.

— Yessir, Mr Captain sir.

Q stamps on the brakes and slides the Cortina to a stop. The malevolent red eye stares back at us, watches us. Ever present. The red light, the line you're not allowed to cross. The place where you have to stop. Deadline, edge of the envelope, cross her and you depart into uncontrolled flight. Turn my head and lock eyes with a glassy stare. Radii looking back at me. Shiny silver number on his shoulder. Look at it, so bright, how it slips and morphs into a mouth, fanged and demented. Waiting to pounce. Stare back, look into the eyes. Head still nodding to the bass. Q whispers frantically.

— Don't look at him. Don't hot it up.

And I, caught like a doe in headlights (before I'm mown down and made into so much dog food), stare back. The beat is in my blood, no losing it now. Watch his eyes narrow, see the cogs start to churn in his head. 3 black youths in a car going where? Must have drugs on them. Must be criminals! Haul them over. Make them empty their pockets. Show them who's boss. Who's in control. See his eyes, Aryan and blue and clear. Cold blue, like the sky in summertime, when the sun's shining bright and everyone's out getting a tan, except those of us who have a permanent year-round tan. I'm always surprised by how white people can hate us so much, yet put themselves through so much pain and financial struggle to disappear for two weeks so they can try to become as black as me.

But the eyes stare at me, cutting through my deflection of thought. I stare back, I'm not dropping my gaze. I ain't no slave, believe that. No backing down. The music holds me in place as time slows, bouncing energy all through me. Ain't nothing going to worry me. Look, wink, smile, grin, then turn away: no confrontation. Defuse it, the demon don't scare me.

We pull away from the lights and Q's forced to settle in behind the PO-LICE van, which travels along sedately in front of us, daring us to do over 30. Daring us to pull out and try to overtake so they can turn on the lights and flag us down. Pull over 3 more niggas, it'll be fun. Pull us over because we're not as pale as them and we don't listen to House. The new DJ's pushing in some Hardcore tracks, going to the stack with the old skool Jungle flavour – if you can call two years *old*.

Q's getting even more anxious, he knows he can't do anything stupid because they'll pull him over quicker than spit. He starts to chew his cheek. Bad sign. I'm waiting, waiting. Watching the back of the van sway in front of us. Our lights illuminating those two blacked-out windows staring sightlessly at us. Daring us to go for it, to try and make a break for it. Winking at us. No place to go, nowhere to hide. They're on the same road and all we can do is follow.

It's a miracle to me that they catch any real criminals with the amount of time they spend harassing us. Just like buses: when you want one, not one to be seen for miles around, then when you couldn't care less about seeing one again they come busting down the street five at once – sitting in a Ford Transit van, travelling at exactly 30 mph directly in front of you. Q's got the radio turned up like a fucker but it ain't doing him no good. He's still sweating.

I remember when he first started driving his mum's car, he took us for a spin around Battersea Park. A clear cold winter's day. We managed to get him to take us inside the park. Drove through the gates and sped down the lanes. We got caught on a patch of black ice and spun into this Merc. No damage to the old lady's rusty old Cortina (we were only doing about 10 or 15 mph), but we left a fucking huge great dent in the side of that Merc. Q pulled away like he'd just run over someone and was drunk at the time. He didn't drive the old dear's motor for a good two years. He still gets serious about it when we bring it up. You can still see that Merc parked opposite Battersea Park with the dent still in its side. I piss myself laughing every time I remember Q's expression: his eyes big and wide, transfixed by the thought of what had happened, what he had done; his mouth open and catching flies. While we were in the back screaming for him to get going, to drive, drive, drive before someone saw us there. Pushing him into action, then Q slowly putting the car into gear and trundling away, with us looking all round, waiting in fear for some irate owner to come running out and take down our licence number and send it to the police. We were running scared for a good few weeks after that, waiting for the police to phone Q's house and inform his mum about how much insurance she would be paying out.

The memory slides out of focus as I watch the police van slow for another set of lights – the brake lights just as malevolent as the lights that they are stopping for. I wonder when my perception of the police changed, from being happy school bobby, nice man who you ran to meet when you were in need of protection, to evil, soul-taking, ignorant, petty, power-hungry racists. Maybe it was when Raymond, Hugie and Johnathon got hauled up Oxford St because some white youth had got mugged and said some black boys did it, identifying Raymond and his posse as the perpetrators even though they'd only just got off the tube. Took them to the police station and locked them up for the rest of the day, even though they knew they hadn't done nothing. Strip searched them and everything else. Maybe that was the turning point – or any of the other times friends would come in and recount stories of harassment and discrimination from the boys in blue. Raymond was never the same. Starting hating all white people, getting into fights, kicking teachers off the bus and basically acting like a wild thing. Last thing I'd heard he was doing time for assault and battery.

The police ain't for shit, they ain't doing me no favours, just putting me under pressure 24/7. I know we're gonna get hauled over, I can feel it in my water. So I start to roll one last joint. When we do get pulled over I'll get done for possession, Q'll get fucked for driving without insurance, and Biggie'll get done cause he's in the car with both of us. My fingers are nervous and shabby as I carefully roll it, lick the gummed edge and try not to lose too much as the car moves on the road. Seal it, roll a roach and twist the open end. Put it into my mouth and hold it there as I search through my pockets for my lighter.

— What are you doing? Take that shit out of your mouth, you're gonna get us pulled over.

— They're gonna pull us over anyway. So I might as well go down fighting.

— We won't get pulled over if you take that shit out of your mouth.

I ignore Q and keep searching. I find the lighter, it's slipped between the cushions covering the back seat. As I pull it out, the van's lights start going. Blue, swirling, rotating beacons of justice. Pointing me out, searchlight, uncovering my crime. Indicator comes on as they cut across two lanes of traffic, pulling a U-turn. As the transit slides away and behind us over on the other side of the road I almost drop the spliff in relief, but check myself, and my shaking hands manage to get the lighter to work. I light it and inhale deeply, winding down my window. I don't want Q's mum thinking her son's a puffhead. I pull it down deep into my lungs and exhale.

— Anyone want a smoke?

Craig Sings

I imagine this time around, she's here, we kiss, we talk, we're pushing the conversation along. I remember her kiss, I remember fucking her, I think that's a mistake, things were just easy.

Now I imagine I'm amongst the many women in my life – I miss you all. All the while my shit mounts, the tears will never come to my cheeks, still I can lie. I look among the smiling faces and try to remember the times when I loved you but I can't see it, I did; I think, time's up. Between a rock and a hard place I've lived and died, I've taken my final turn and it had better be freedom. For up against Daddy (Nova Daddy), I am a bird, free to fly while animals play. I look among the smiling faces and try to remember the times when I loved *her* and I am not very sure. I remember you suckled me to sleep and I held my breath, then I said goodbye to the night. You used to lie next to me but you could have been light years away. Night slowly turns to day. Hours of talk can reverse years of pain, but you never listened, you never cared. The sting in the scorpion's tail, the paradox, is that hate softens with the years, but the blade is warmed when the cold steel is fed fresh blood. I can see the concrete drying on my tombstone and my name set in stone, yet still I'm all alone, 'cause no one goes when I go. When I'm an angel I'll spread my wings like an eagle, shield my babies from the rain, shield them from the pain, make right what's insane.

Shout Out

— This is the 0956, the 123, the 321. Style FM waiting for your shout outs. Come wid dem. The studio massive in full effect, this one goes out to you. Last caller call back.

— *Jason from Hammersmith don't know what you're chatting about. Big up your chess.*

— The 0956, the 123, the 321.

— *Big shout out to Michael in Clapham from the Boogie massive, out there in Hounslow.*

— *Big shout out to Emma from Frankie and all the Pimlico massive, living large and taking charge.*

— Style FM. 105.3 FM. We ain't going out like that . . . Ruff, ruff. Wheel! Wheel! My DJ. The man like Megatron on the ones and twos. Bad bwoy tune. Come again, selector. When Bad bwoy get drop, man know we have to take it from the top. Big up your chess, all the Jungle massive. Time to get hyper. Time to get hyper.

— *Big shout to Mandy from the Pirate posse out there in Dalston.*

— You know the number: the 0956, the 123, the 321. Keep it locked to the style FM. 105.3 . . . OH GOSH!!! My god! Megatron, run dat one again . . . Just for you London, the heavy dub plate pressure of the man like Megatron. Big up your chess . . . Dis tune going out to all them like pussy face sound bwoy who go on like dem wear bullet proof vess, but know dem can't tess.

Craig. *T.R.O.Y.*

I reminisce, I reminisce . . .

The street lights glow outside, a warm gentle orange, spilling illumination through and onto me as I lie in my bed, looking at the ceiling, wondering. Stretch my arm as it's getting tired and cramped from being underneath my head. Weary, I turn onto my side and curl up, feel the empty space and smell Anna there. She's been gone for 3 months and I can still smell her everywhere, sharp and all-pervading. I can just close my eyes and see her face. Eyes closed, mouth open, teeth showing. Lips parted as she holds me close and whispers my name in my ear. Breathing it heavy, sensuous. Her breath rolling across my ear, as I throb and shudder.

Open my eyes and stare at the space that she isn't in. Drag my body upwards and run my hand over my picky afro. Want her to be here, but know she won't be. Got to live with her not being here all the time. Know she's gone away to do what she is happiest doing, gaining knowledge and experience, and I didn't just want to be hanging around getting angry that I wasn't enjoying myself, not doing what I wanted to do. Scared that just being with her wouldn't be enough. That we'd split apart. So now I just wait for her, go through the motions of living, forgetting what I do from day to day and living life in a hazy fog, thick and cloying, softening the sensation of living.

Whip the quilt off me. I'm restless, too much energy. I know what I don't want to do but not what I want to do. I don't feel like listening to the radio or watching TV. I roam the flat, searching for some ease. I sit, stand, lie. Trying to get comfortable somewhere, somehow, and in the trying just make myself more restless. Finally I come to a stop at the computer. Stare down at it for long seconds. She bought it so that we'd always be in touch, not just through speaking on the phone, but by putting our thoughts down in a slower, more thoughtful way. She knows I type faster than I write, it's why she got it, so I wouldn't have to spend long hours writing a letter long hand when I could just churn it out quickly typing. So it's sat here for the past three months, unused, gathering dust except for the odd game of solitaire or Maelstrom. Pause and wonder if this is what I want to be doing. Close my eyes and see if sleep will overtake me. Lean forward and switch it on, the brightness of the screen as it lights up causing me to blink rapidly to adjust. Plug in the modem and hunch myself forward, peering at the letters as they appear.

one

> my fingers probe your moistness,
> your wetness,
> know your head is thrown back, mouth open.
> low sounds emerging from your throat.
> my hands cup you,
> slides across, finger searching, probing.
> lips open,
> fingers spread inside, liquid opening, finger
> tickles.
> drag my hand through the soft moistness,
> across the tight curls up to your belly button.
> innie or outie?
> innie. my finger delves, creating a pool of fluid,
> soft, inviting, waiting.

two

> how many times have i sat with you?
> just looking.
> watching the way you move,

the way your weight balances on your bones,
your frame.
skin, hair, mouth – soft and fertile, moist.
your eyes, liquid deep, knowing.
the skin at your throat beckons.
it calls me.
siren song.
i know to place my lips upon it will close your
    eyes,
part your lips, bring your hand up to cradle my
    head,
caress my nape.
fingers trailing along my spine

three

exploration,
chance, to find the sensitive,
touch, stroke, caress.
strangely complicated but ultimately simple.
fingers, lips.
sense of touch, smell.
hearing, seeing, being,
talking, speaking.
where to touch, push, rub.
how hard, soft.
one finger, two.
whole hand smoothing a path.
penetrate,

flesh inside flesh.
tongue on tongue,
mouth across mouth.
sitting, lying, standing,
breathing hard across my face.
shadows, night, no light.
skin, flesh exposed, concealed.
ticklish.
your tongue across
fingers along
concentration,
detachment overridden.
passion, desire. no longer apart from,
apart of. spasm.
i move she moves, rhythm,
black out, cessation.
until next time.

four

long time no see,
eyes soft and dark, pupils expanding,
drinking me in.
soft,
so very soft. touch.
fingers trailing down your spine.
skin so smooth to touch.
reach the base, slide
gently

backstreets

down the
crevice,
dark unknown.
feel your weight on me,
feel your breath on me.
take me in.
hold me in.
never let me go.
never.
try to deny,
instinctively know.
better to go,
to leave.
an agony of wanting,
desire raging with reason,
perceptions bent,
warped,
twisted.
good or bad.
in the balance. delirium.
la lune goddess of the moon,
lunacy. is it. 70% water.
tide, hi or low, affect me, affect her.
pupils always tiny,
a
severing, mental from emotional,
passionless,
emotionless, non dilation. pregnancy.
intoxication,

infatuation,
supplication.
kneel, tongue extended, pray.

I sit back and rub my eyes, suddenly tired, a yawn forcing itself from my mouth. I stretch and press the send button, spilling my demented ramblings down the line to her in Martinique. Teaching, reading, being. I stare at the screen for a second and try to figure out where all of the words come from. They don't sound like me. They rise and fall with their own cadences and rhythm. She always said she loved to read what I wrote, but I stopped a while ago. Dreaming on paper's not the same as making money. It was one or the other so I sacrificed the writing. Didn't think it would make a difference, not in the line of work that I'm in. But I sit and feel at ease for the first time since she's left. As if just by the mere act of writing I have placed my feelings onto paper and can now move on, past what was affecting me, worrying me. I used to do that when I was younger, write everything that was affecting me onto a sheet of paper, vent my anger through the action of writing, then screw it up and chuck it away and feel immediately better.

I lean forward and turn off the machine, ready for sleep now. Restless no more.

Groove Thang

Alex's place is big, lots of space. He's left the sofa and some chairs in and pushed them over against one of the curving walls. As Wayne says in *Wayne's World*,—*Cool, this is the kind of place I'm gonna get when I move out of my parents' house.* It's a round house, no sharp corners anywhere to be seen, and I've always wondered how Alex could afford it. I think maybe he's got rich parents, but I haven't asked him and he hasn't told me.

For the short time that I was in college Alex was my closest friend. Used to hang out all the time – play the arcades, go for drinks, sit and chat about intellectual subjects. Next to Q and Biggie Alex is the closest thing I have to family outside of my family.

His place is on the top floor of a round apartment block in Camden, large windows and a stainless-steel kitchen. The wooden floor is usually covered by rugs but he's moved these out so that people can dance without trampling them to death. Photographs that he's taken strung across his walls printed huge, 30 by 50. The only adornment on his walls. The lights are low and the DJ's in the corner lit by his decks, spinning the tracks that everyone wants to hear. People are speaking as people do at parties: some quiet, some loud, but always in small knots and groups. There's a gradual migration to the centre of the room, the space made for the dancefloor.

Everyone's about their mid 20s and it seems as if we're the youngest ones here. I'm clutching my glass and speaking gently to Q about why I was smoking in his mum's car when Alex pops over. Flame-red hair long and spiky, creating a halo around him. He's tall and angular, lean and wolf-like as he leans over us, his eyes sparkling.

— Meth, I didn't think you were going to make it.

He swallows me up into a huge hug and I'm worried about losing my drink down his back. I hold him tight to me and feel the warmth that only friends and family create. He holds me at arm's length and laughs the heavy wheezing laugh that he's carried with him as long as I've known him. The bluff Yorkshireman he used to be still visible under the surface now and then.

— You know me, Alex: Undercover Elephant. Let me introduce my friends, Biggie and Q.

— Pleased to meet you. Have you got drinks? Good, let's go and socialise.

He drags me away on his arm and spins me into the crowd that is mingling. I feel out of my depth as Alex takes me on a whirlwind tour of all the people at the party, names and faces bleeding into a blur. A squashed mess of colour. Alex is the butterfly host, flitting from one group to another, leaving a joke here, a joke there, being at the centre of the conversation but also on the edge. Before I know it I'm back with Q and Biggie, standing once more on the edge as Alex sails off to be Alex once more.

— What's with him?

— Alex is an actor. Right now he's playing the part of the perfect host.

I look around and see a space become available on the sofa. I'm in like Flynn, shoving my butt on to it and pulling my gear out of my jacket pocket while sipping on my Southern Comfort and lemonade with ice. Don't you just love drinks with long names? I surely do. I sip at it leisurely as Q and Biggie step delicately over, standing above me, nodding their heads to Flava in ya ear. Drinks held at their sides, hands in pockets, looking uncomfortable. The only thing keeping them here is me and the fact that the food and drink are free and the music is good. The big speakers he's got in are pumping out clear pure sound, but at the moment working well below capacity as Alex allows people to mingle and talk as well as dance.

I nod my head in time to the off-cadence rhyming scheme as I lick half of a gummed edge and stick my two papers together. The woman sitting next to me stands up, knocking me slightly, and doesn't even say *excuse me* as she saunters off. I'm giving her butt the evil eye as Q slides in beside me and Biggie decides now's the right time to make a play for a honey who's standing all on her lonesome, looking out the window at the night below.

— Why do you smoke so much?

I look up from sprinkling my grass into the joined kingsize Rizlas to look at Q's earnest face. He's being serious now, no bullshitting. So I tell him the truth.

— I like feeling stoned, when everything slows down and you can just float away. It's a damn good feeling. But the best thing about it is I'm still myself, I'm not tripping or speeding or loving everyone to death. I'm just doing me things but in a mellow way.

I lick down the side of a cigarette. Silk Cut ultra low tar. Tear the wet strip away and sprinkle half the contents of the cigarette into the rizla, twisting the ragged paper back around the cigarette so the tobacco doesn't fall out when it's back in the packet.

— Why?

Q looks down at his hands, sits up and leans forward, rubs his nose for a second, then stares at me.

— I don't know. I want to know what it feels like.

I'm loading the roach into the end now and carefully tapping with a finger to pick any missed fragments so I can slide them into the open end. Having got as much in as possible – not that there was much floating around – I twist the end and insert the spliff into my mouth.

— Have you ever smoked a cigarette?

— No. You know I haven't.

— Smoking a cigarette is like smoking a joint.

Your head goes light, it goes cold, experiences seem that much sharper and it's sort of like being drunk, yet not, at the same time. Spliffs give you that, but they also mellow you out – make everything easier, not so much of a rush or a hassle. You just feel calmer all the way around.

I take out my lighter and hold it reflectively in my hands. A Zippo. *Going on a Zippo raid, Sarge. Well make sure and burn down some gook village for me, son. Do it for me, son. Burn one for the Gipper.* I've always wanted one, I just love the sound they make – and the act of opening it is so cool. I suppose it's why I've got a jack knife as well, I just love flicking things open.

— Do you want to try it?

Q looks at me uncertainly and I'm sure he's going to say no, just by the look on his face, as if I've just told him to eat shit.

— Emily says I don't take enough risks, that I'm safe – which is what attracted me to her. That I need to lighten up, stop being so serious. How is smoking a spliff going to make me act less serious?

— I ain't the world's greatest expert on love and sex and women and all that stuff but leave her well enough alone. Any woman that wants to change you don't really want you, she wants some fake-ass magazine construction.

Q looks unsure of this. His face was tortured as he told me what he'd been holding in for so long. Anal sex – getting it or not – was the least of his problems. I light my joint and puff on it, getting it to burn smooth, taking a few quick drags, blow out smoke and hold it out to Q. He looks at me, then slowly takes it from my hand.

— Don't laugh if I start coughing.

— Just inhale and pull it deep into your lungs, hold it there then let it out nice and slow.

He puts it to his mouth and makes a huge O with his lips before taking a tentative drag and blowing it out very quickly. He tries again and holds it down for longer, his eyes watering as the smoke wafts into them. Takes another drag and takes it down, holds it for a long second, then breathes it out. I see his body start to relax almost immediately. His eyes take on a hooded look as his lids lower. His hand rises slowly to his mouth and he drags deep, expelling the smoke in a long stream as if he's been doing this for years.

— You've done this before, haven't you?

He gives a little-boy grin and passes it back to me. I wave it away and start building another one, letting him get really stoned. We weren't going to drive back tonight anyway.

— I was like Bill Clinton, I smoked one but I never inhaled.

This sends him into a fit of the giggles, trying to hide his mouth behind his hand without burning his nose with the spliff.

Lonely Hearts

I slide off the chair and over to her. She's gorgeous: large eyes, rosebud mouth, with a luscious bottom lip. Breasts pert but full, stretching her top, long bare legs beneath a short skirt and, what's best, bare feet encased in Reebok classics.

— Hi!

She turns away from looking down on the city. Immediately I make eye contact with her. Being honest and truthful. She looks at me, as if asking why I'm doing this. She doesn't know me: Why should she talk to me? This is always the hardest part — getting a woman to talk to you for more than a minute without her just shaking her head, or giving a simple yes or no answer. You have to structure your questions so that you get more than one-word answers. This is especially difficult if you're coming in cold when she hasn't made eye contact before letting you know that she's interested, because you're trying to get to her before someone else does.

— My name's Biggie, what's yours?

A simple answer to a simple question is all I require at this point, just to let me know whether she's interested or not.

— I don't really want to talk right now.

She's being blatant, hoping that her being frosty is enough to make me disappear back to whichever part of the room I appeared from. She's turned her head away already, gone back to looking out of the wide expanse of glass window. I lean forward and put my head next to hers and look out at what she's looking at. Turn my head and whisper into her ear.

— Do you like chocolate?

This makes her think. Women like chocolate like men like football: if allowed to run unchecked it can become an obsession. I know this. I live in a house full of women and it's shown me what is needed to gain access to a woman's heart and through that, her pussy. Chocolate is a powerful tool to be used only sparingly. After she's thought for maybe a second she gives me the what-do-you-take-me-for look, and turns away again. I retreat back into honesty.

— OK so you don't want to speak to me, that's fine.

I smile then just to put her at ease.
— But I would like to speak to you when you're more willing. Look, here's my number, if you get the desire to eat chocolate, you know who to call.

I slip the ready-written number onto the sill in front of her and turn away back to Meth and Q. Right now she's thinking furiously about what just happened, trying to figure out which angle I'm playing, wondering if it's worth it. I've left the ball in her court because I didn't ask for her number, I gave her mine. Makes her think, makes her decide. Gives her the power in a situation like this to say yes or no, rather than just saying no all the time because you just don't want to be harassed anymore. I can see her thinking about it, trying not to look at the number.

See the night reflecting off her olive skin. She's half-caste and even as the word's travelling into my head I slip it to *mixed race*. Fuck being politically correct, but half-caste is almost as bad as being called a nigga. And it pisses me off this incessant debate about skin tone. Why does it make so much fucking difference? We're all the same under the skin, we can all have sex with whoever, cutting out all cultural and religious differences. Physically we can create babies with anyone regardless of their skin tone. There is no such thing as race, for there is only the human race, and we are all part of it.

It just burns me when all people can think about is whether you're going out with a white girl or not, or a white guy or not. Having white blood in you, having black blood in you, as if you can tell how black a person is just by looking at their complexion. It is just so dishonest, so fucking dishonest. Live and let live. Why the eternal question: A*m I dark enough*? I*'m too light*. Get the fuck outta here. You are what you are. Just saying I'm only going out with dark-skinned black women is wrong and divisive, it makes people nothing more than a skin tone.

When guys like Meth, who are as dark as fuck, want the light-skinned honeys, because it's closer to white without being white, then give me all that bullshit about jungle fever when I go out with a white girl. It's just so much knob. They're all militant against white people, yet they are willing to overlook the white blood in their girlfriends just because they've been brought up in a black environment, and act black, and talk black. But don't they think that mixed-race people are as confused as anyone else about what is happening? Do they feel comfortable in black surroundings with black people, or do they feel more at ease with white people, because their blackness is not questioned, they know where they stand, whereas with black people there is always going to be the stigma of having a white parent and in so doing, just not being black enough.

People have to understand that sexual desire and physical attraction have no conventions, obey no restrictions. Why else would slave-owners who have their own white wives go out into the fields to have sex with black women? Now if I was a slave never having seen a white person before, I would have thought they were piss ugly, and vice versa. So what drove these slave-owners to spread their seed far and wide with our ancestors, making light-skinned children then shoving the blame for their own desires onto black women, creating this myth about them being wanton and always ready, just as they reconstructed the black male into this sex-hungry, big-dicked animal who lusts after white flesh?

All skin tone proves is that if you live near the equator you have dark skin, light skins towards the poles and yellows and browns in between. The differences are climatic but they have been transformed into genetics.

All this thinking is doing my head in. I can't get my head around it. I know my point of view and where I stand, I'll go out with any girl if I'm attracted to her, and everyone else can spin on a sharp stake slowly. I take a sip of my drink – rum and coke – and move over to where Q is sitting, head back, dying spliff in his hand, with Meth quietly and efficiently making another on his lap.

— I hope you know what you're doing.

The Anamorphic Q

I slide deeper into the seat and feel the drug swirl around my head. Images come unbidden as my conscious mind slips away. Aware of the sounds around me but my unconscious pushing through, making things stand out as if my lens was out of focus and has now been pulled back sharply into clarity.

Beauty lay within the court-room and instructed me to follow my own road. I asked her where true beauty could be found and she led me through forests and deserts. We flew under water and over air, travelled through rich and poor, spoke to charming animals, attractive people. We wandered and ran — to nowhere — and returned to the court. Then she left me alone years away from my true home. So I left and returned to the elements looking for true beauty. I roamed again until at the furthest point to which I had ever travelled. I stopped. All around was blackness. A deep, shiny, domineering dark. And in an instant I transcended my own mind and started a journey within, lasting time. I was waking up. The darkness *darkened and awareness fell like dawn. I returned again to the physical to discover beauty at its highest. It was all the same except I felt everything in technicolour. I heard birds singing for miles and smelled the buzzing plants. It was all beautiful but nothing paralleled the beauty I had found in my own court-room.*

I slip back into intelligible thought. I haven't dreamt in a long time. Well, I know I still dream, it's just that I don't remember them. When I was younger I used to dream about being a racing driver, recurring images of myself at the wheel of a very fast Formula 1 car, racing down a long straight. I used to dream it every night on and off for about 7 months. Then I stopped and never dreamt it again. I still don't know why I dreamt it in the first place. I was thirteen at the time and susceptible to all kinds of influences. Try not to worry too much about what might have been. Right now I'm reading English and History at university and trying to keep my head above water in this relationship. Emily just seems to be swamping me and I feel that I'm losing too much of myself.

I don't have to look down to know the spliff's dead, its lighted end no longer glowing, now black and smoky.

This is what I mean. Before I met Emily this would never have happened, but I can't be sure that it wasn't going to happen anyway. Can't be sure that this rebel in me wasn't there all along. That I was going to smoke dope and slip into intoxicating sexual relationships. Just thinking about Emily makes me stiff in my pants. It appears so quickly I'm immediately uncomfortable and trying to shift my position. So doing I open my eyes and find Biggie blowing smoke into my nostrils, grinning as he does it. I smile to show that I'm not offended and not likely to rip his head off.

When Alex returns.

— Budge up, Meth. Skinning up without me. That's deplorable.

— You know me: roll that shit, light that shit, smoke it.

Alex slides in beside Meth and happily wraps his arm around his shoulder, smiling beatifically into our faces, his gaze slipping away into the distance, watching people's faces. Since I've been away in dreamland the DJ's slipped into another set: cool swing, Jodeci, voices sighing in harmony as the chorus comes in. The dancefloor is becoming slightly packed, with couples swaying together, arms locked tight around each other's bodies. Reminds me of Valentine's Day. Reminds me of Emily. Alex bends down, his nimble fingers, quickly rolling another spliff even as

Meth is bringing his to his lips, Zippo at the ready. Biggie's looking up at the ceiling as he tries to blow smoke rings with his half-finished joint. I hold out my hand and he looks surprised for an instant, then passes it over.

— Don't smoke all of it.

— So. What happened to you and the girl then?

— Nothing. I gave her my number and we'll see what we shall see.

— How do you do it? How do you get all those girls?

— You just talk to them – as human beings, rather than holes for your dick.

— That simple?

— Yep.

I can feel myself slipping away. The spliff's just too much for me, I can feel my senses sliding into other realms. Close my eyes and it feels as if I'm moving into hyperspace, constantly jumping towards and through objects in the distance, my whole field of vision taken in by that slanting square of movement. I wonder if this is what it feels like to be tripping. But from what I've heard that's like total sensory overload.

Open my eyes and bend down for the drink, but I can't find it. It's down there I know and my hand's searching around. I don't want to lean forward in case I fall off the sofa, so I hunt around for another few minutes, with Biggie looking at me very strangely indeed. Feel my hand hit a cold glass, clutch it to me and hold it up. My eyes are going hyperspace on me as I jump towards the glass, then through the glass, then into the orange juice, then through the other side of the glass and towards the window. Quickly take a sip and wipe my hand over my face and sit very quietly, hoping that the feeling will go away if I don't move. I drink the juice, not feeling the intoxication lessen, but the clammy dirty feeling that had been in my mouth for a while disappears as the juice slides down my throat. I find that now I actually want to smoke some more, so I bring the spliff to my lips and take another toke.

Be a Child of Your Time

Alex doesn't bother to put any tobacco into his spliff, just fills it up with grass, pulling out a wooden box about the size of a cigarette packet and sprinkling his grass onto his papers. Rolls it swiftly and lights it. Taking long pulls on it. Letting his body become looser, more sinuous. Offers it to me and I look at the spliff in my hand and the temptation is too much. I pass mine along to Biggie, who's watching Q get more and more stoned. Take a drag and sit there feeling it rush across my chest and up to my brain. Wash out, riding the waves of experience and sensation. Alex has got his head on his hand and is looking at me, a smile in his eyes as he watches me smoke.

— What? What?

— Nothing. I just like watching you smoke, so delicate. You know Meth, when you smoke you show your true self. No masks, no covering, just the bare essentials.

I look at him. This is one of Alex's well known tangents, slipping away into some topic of conversation which makes no sense whatsoever except to himself. I suppose it's one of the reasons I like him so much. I see a lot of me in him.

— Next I suppose you'll be telling me that looking through a person's record collection is like looking through their underwear draw.

— How did you guess? Are you telepathic?

I blow smoke in his face just to let him know I know that he's not being serious, and pull myself to my feet. The DJ's playing I *Wanna Be Down*, the intro rolling through.

— I'm gonna dance.

I move very gingerly into the crowded ruck of bodies now swaying in front of the sofa, knowing I won't have a seat to go back to once the song's done. The vocals are soft and gentle as I close my eyes and listen to the song, doing my soul dance, back and forth, one foot out, one foot back. Click my fingers, take another drag on my joint. The undiluted grass wafts in a stream out of my mouth into the already smoke-filled air.

Beneath my lids I see the music drifting on the breeze of motion created by our dancing. I feel lonely. I want some female company, but I can't be bothered to step to a girl. So much hard work and graft. What would be really nice is if a girl stepped to me. But that ain't never gonna happen. The only girls that step to me are either drunk, ugly or both. The pretty ones just stand and wait, passive princesses waiting for that knight in shiny white armour to come and speak to them. So when the ugly bastard from around the way steps forth because he's secure in his ugliness and doesn't mind chatting pure rubbishness in her ear for a long while, she takes him and then stays with him for the next 5 years of her life, just because he stepped to her. Life is ultimately unfair, whichever way you spin it. If you play spin bottle, you'll kiss the ugly ho at the other end. It's inevitable.

I dance through the smoke, clicking my fingers and smoking Alex's joint slowly, savouring the intoxication it brings on. I *Wanna Be Down* slides into *Creep* and I enjoy the mix. The DJ's good, knows his stuff. I find that I'm drifting over to the window and let myself get pushed over in that direction, going with the flow. I stand there for an instant and am surprised by how large the moon is tonight. Maybe it's something in the water. The music plays on, soft and seductive, voices silky smooth as the words glide through me.

La Lune

Mistress of my heart, controller of my destiny. How I yearn for you, burn for you. I want to be encircled in your embrace, through the cold winter nights. Your form above me in the heavens as I stare at you. Desiring you always and forever desiring you. Desiring to be close to you. When the sun goes down, where are you? Who knows where you appear from. I want you all around me, through me. No more sitting in the dark and waiting for you. La Lune, rise above me and let me feel you. Let me touch you, know you, thrill you. I wish to know the pleasures of you, pleasures that no earthly delights can sustain. La Lune.

Afro

Mr Meth

I wake up and I'm not sure where I am for a long time. My eyes search for a familiar landmark, some point of reference that will shift me into a stratum of existence where I'm aware of what's around me. Planes, levels within levels, overlaying things, my points of view shifted out of whack, out of gear. Toothed gears crunching against one another, making a whole heap of noise. My eyes are burning and I feel the need for some cover. Light is pouring in from every angle and my whole view is tipped upside down. My eyes slowly open, but I'm not seeing anything. Nothing is familiar, nothing is mine. I'm trying to make sense of it. Rolling over onto my front so that everything's level is a good start.

It's a big room. I'm lying on a sofa that's pushed hard up against a curved wall. In fact the whole room is curved. Some decks laid on a high worktable sit next to some big speakers over on the other side of the room and next door to the speakers is a huge expanse of glass. A window on the world from which all of the light is emanating. Cover my eyes and stagger over to the decks just to see whether the DJ's left some records as well. In the process find that I'm only wearing my boxers and that I'm holding rather tightly to a blanket, which trails behind me. Even when my senses are making no sense to me whatsoever, my brain has enough gusto to keep me covered. For some reason that makes me laugh and I fall into a laughing fit as I hold myself up at the window.

The view is different from the one I know. Higher up and showing a lot more. Long rows of houses, curving off into the distance. Tall tower blocks shafting like spears into the sky as if some giant has left his spade in the ground. My eyes squinting hard against the light, I turn my head away and look for shelter, still unsure of where I am. I'm not really a morning person, it always takes me several hours to get into a day, several hours and enough coffee to keep South American coffee producers financially stable forever. My clothes are crumpled up in a heap on the floor next to the sofa and I can't be bothered to put them on just yet.

Wrapping the blanket around my waist I move slowly from the front room into the kitchen. Unsure how I know where this stainless-steel monstrosity was supposed to be. It's almost as bright in here as it is in the front room. The venetian blind is split open, letting long slashes of light through. I turn on the kettle and retreat to the toilet, my bladder desperately needing release. It's only as I stand in front of the toilet that my mind kicks back into gear. Watching the hands on the ornate clock above my head tick around to half 4.

This is Alex's place. We must have crashed here last night. I shake the last drips from my little soldier and put it back into my boxers, reaching over to pull the musical toilet chain. As I head back to the kitchen and the stainless steel reflecting light like a diamond, I'm still trying to figure out how I lost the last 8 hours in my life. I don't even remember going to sleep or anything. Nobody's in the flat, but there's a note on the front door telling me to use the spare key and that everyone will be back around six. Sip my very strong, very black coffee and pull my clothes on, heading out of the door quickly and down into Camden. Never really like Camden too tuff, it's a bit pretentious for my liking, too much up its own arse. I prefer Brixton or Streatham. Clapham's a bit iffy, but Camden just got a bit too much . . . I don't know, I think it takes itself too seriously.

Going out again tonight. Got to look good, got to look sharp. Find a barber's – that's what's at the top of my list. And after wandering through huge waves of shoppers, like a crowd of football supporters spilling out of the ground, heading for the markets, I'm starting to feel very aggrieved. When I do find one it's just around the corner from where Alex lives (if I'd gone right instead of left I would have seen it almost immediately). I'm a bit taken out by the prices. Cutting hair is cutting hair, the next thing you know they'll be charging 15 quid for a short back and sides.

I step through the glass door into an area where magic still lives. What is it about the barber and the magic that he wields over us who sit in the chair? I'm like the only customer. It must be a really slow day, it's not usually this quiet on a Saturday afternoon. The emptiness of the place shocks me for a while: maybe this barber is really bad and he's going to destroy my hair. But I've only come to have it all shaved off anyway, so there's no big deal.

I sit in the leather seat and feel the magic weave around me. The rustle of the cape being pulled tight under the chin. The electric hum as the clippers stroke across my scalp, the back of the neck, my ear pulled down. Hair falling gently along the nape. The constant electrical hum that resonates within the eardrums: an ode to drowsiness, with the ability to pronounce a sentence of tractability on anyone who sits within the chair. For those minutes in the magic chair I'll make no sound except to answer when a quiet question is asked, make no movement except for those that he asks for. Head down, as if in prayer, supplication to a barber god. The strong sure hands, moving my head this way, that way. Gentle pressure, gentle strength.

The hairs lie on my cheek, on my eyelids, held from my eye by the soft, gently-moving lashes that wave there. Snorted breath from mouth or nose has no effect, the hairs stay unmoving and resplendent in their ability to irritate in such tranquil surroundings. Sleeping almost as I sit, feeling detached from reality, hypnotised into immobility by the drone of the clippers. The quick and urgent sounds of the scissors as they pass lightly along the hairs.

Pauses: some long, some short. Waiting, hardly breathing, waiting for that soft, white, long-haired brush to be lifted from the shrine of instruments, creams and lotions on the shelf in front of me. My reflection bears no resemblance to the person who sat in the chair those long moments ago.

The talcum powder, sweet smelling and

angelic, floated softly onto the brush. It is swished gently across the back of the neck – quickly, surely, expertly. Another flick of the wrist pulling it slowly along the path already traversed. A finger pulling my collar away. The cape that has captured all of my hair is pulled off, and the chair swivelled with a flourish. Look in the mirror, nod, smile: satisfied.

Blowing Through

A quick tilt of my head, hands thrown high, dipping my shoulder, pimp limp in effect. Jerky yet rhythmic, off key, slanted off kilter. Method Man on some shit.

I'm foul an' I'm sick,
And I'm coming for that headpiece proteck it.

Don't you just love black music? I'm walking over to the car, all fired up for going out. The Cortina is sitting there beside the kerb, as if it's done something wrong. A dog that's just been told it's bad. Time to blow through. Q and Biggie are moving in front of me as I wave my hands, generally acting like a madman.

Night has swept through again, painting its dark self over everything. The stars twinkling in the dark sky. Look up and watch Orion's belt and the Big Dipper. Those are the only two that I know, but I'm always amazed when I find them time after time, as if they'd disappear on me. Q chucks himself into the car, slamming the front door as he always does, and I wonder how last night affected him. He's made a radical shift away from who he was for a woman, and that's always bad news. I try not to think about Cassie at this point. I'm still taken by surprise by the force of emotion that charges forth at the mention of her name.

I'm sitting in the car thinking about her, listening to the wind finding cracks within the body shell. Thinking these deep thoughts and wondering as I always have whether I made the right choice. Cassie: she was my first love. Bright, intelligent, funny and she loved all of me, all the time. I loved her as much as I was able to.

For 17 years I'd trained myself to hold everything inside: I couldn't allow anyone inside me. No one could see the real me, the emotional me, the child that cried during *Kramer vs Kramer*. The child who felt betrayed when his closest friend in school spat out the secret I'd gifted him within the middle of an argument. Cassie got inside me and stayed inside me for the duration. She was my first love. I was just out of my first 2 sexual relationships, looking for more lust, not any deep meaningful into-the-bloodstream, full-on, going-steady thing. But that's what I got.

I met her at a party in Brixton. She was standing alone (her friends had deserted her for a second) and she was getting charged from every direction. I think she saw me as an easy out, and I wasn't getting heavy or nothing, I was just in one of those any-girl-in-this-room-will-succumb-to-my-charms moods when I felt nothing would stand in my way. We talked, found out that we were very similar. I walked her home, tried to get into her panties and she blanked me. I didn't mind, she wouldn't give me her number, so I gave her mine and forgot about it until she phoned me 4 weeks later.

From then on it was a descent into that madness called love. She infuriated me, she drove me crazy, but I always wanted to be with her. And she always loved me, that was never in doubt. Then I got scared. Nothing was the same, everything was changed. I wasn't the same, I felt differently all the way around, and then I couldn't handle it anymore, so I broke it clean and quick. Except it wasn't.

It broke my heart. Turned me into a quivering crying wreck. I just wanted to stay in my house and cry, away from everyone and everything. All the emotion I'd kept locked away inside of me was let loose in an intense conflagration. It burned to the core. I don't know where she's gone or what she's doing, but every time I think about her – her laugh, her smile, the way she would hold me close and whisper I *love you* in my ear, then snuggle into my neck as if she was embarrassed – I think maybe she was the one. Maybe I've made the worst mistake of my life and I'll never be as happy ever again.

It haunts me. Sitting on my shoulder, night and day. I was with her for 2 years. It still hurts. I think maybe it always will. Cassie, like every woman, has that strength that women possess, a tough that men can't understand, strong and fragile at the same time. Able to show emotion and be honest about what is going through them, not hiding it deep inside. It's just there, written on their faces, just beneath the surface: this innate ability – maybe it's hormonal – that gives women such inner strength to push through adversity.

I switch my head back on and try to get myself into some fit state to live in. Q's driven away from Camden and I'm not sure when he did it, so deep was I into my own thoughts. I've got to get myself back into that frame of mind I had when I stepped out of Alex's door. I have to delve into myself, search for that feeling of light-headed giddiness. I've got to get it back, or I might as well be staying in my house right now watching some bullshit film on ITV. We're heading for the Lazerdrome and I'm going to enjoy myself.

Q's speeding as he usually does, rushing around London in a broken-down Cortina, listening to the radio. It ain't no jeep and this ain't

Sunset Boulevard, but we still jeeping. Booming sounds firing out of the speakers. Sound swarming around us like bees, swarming like a fucker, getting under your skin. Taking you back to the place where you had so much energy. Putting you back right there. Where the walls were sweating and the women were half-dressed and your cock's rubbed raw from win'ing up on her bottom – or, if the truth be known, standing still while she moves her bottom on your crotch. The music reaching back and tapping that latent pool of energy that has been filled up every time I go raving.

Q takes us around a corner on two wheels and pushes even harder to jump the lights, flashing us towards Peckham.

Heart of Darkness

Saturday night, strobe light on slow, putting the real world on hold, setting yourself free and living in this State of Bass. As a love song has no meaning unless you're in love, a Jungle tune makes no sense unless you're in the jungle. The crowd bursts into verse, on the corner of this world; away from Jazz, Soul, Hip Hop, Techno. Reggae, the smoke creates new dreams, you're travelling through another dimension – a dimension of sight and sound. With the world coming to the end of another century the extinction agenda is almost being set, and all told you feel perhaps this is a comfortable end.

We're here together and it's a party after all.

So a peace was struck, the Irish boyz looked beat up, the niggaz around the way were looking for Craig, and the world was still spinning on the same axis.

The Lazerdrome

The Lazerdrome in deepest, darkest Peckham. Where the bad boys hang out, roaming the streets like so many dark wraiths, waiting to pounce on those unsuspecting enough to come through with no back-up. Peckham's a dump almost as bad as Dalston and it just makes me depressed every time I have to even come near both of those areas. The Lazerdrome, the latest outlet for our weekly Jungle fix, is a converted Quasar arena, now equipped with a huge sound system and lights that wouldn't look out of place on an alien spaceship. It's a maze of walkways and corners, spaces where you can just sit on the floor or dance behind draping designs, away from prying eyes. The chillout room's got a wall which they loop old cartoons on, while nearby they've got some arcade machines for us niggas that haven't forgotten playing R-Type and Space Harrier in our lunch breaks in the local fish and chip shop.

The thing about the Lazerdrome that gets up my nose is the amount of rudeboys who swing in as if they are No. 1 bad boy and ain't no copper gonna take 'em alive when they're still in school and getting put in detention by their history teacher. So fuck the little snot-nosed brats. Just 'cause you like the dark stuff don't mean you know Jungle. They always get on my fucking nerves, screwing up their faces and looking to knife anyone that looks at them for too long, just to create some reputation of being a nutter, a hard man. Don't test him he'll kill you. Well they ain't gonna kill me.

We saunter in and already the dark beats are on top of us. Them hard Ragga lyrics striding into the centre of the arena. The place is heavily male-orientated, which is another thing I don't like about it, as well as having a few speed freaks running like Linford Christie on the beat – eyes wide, frenzied. Just watching them makes me feel exhausted. The rudeboys are striding through the place like they own it, waiting for someone to bump them, spliffs held militant in their fingers, defiant. Waiting for someone to come up to them and tell them to take that shit out of their mouth. Waiting for a chance to prove their masculinity. I leave them to it and head over to the games arena to test my faded re-flexes on some of the games they've got over there. Super Streetfighter II, Killer Instinct, Daytona Racing, Virtual Cop, Mad Dog McCree. The youths are all piled up in front of Killer Instinct, trying out new lethal combinations to destroy their opponents, jostling each other, eyes intent on the screen, mouths one moment tight and grimacing, the next wide and shouting obscenities, cursing their opponent, the character they're playing, the game, everything but their own skill. Rocking the machine back and forth in their desire to win, to prove who is the best, to make themselves superior to their peers. I want to play a game but can't be bothered to get through them. So I leave it for a while and stroll through the place behind Q and Biggie watching faces, weighing up the atmosphere and how everyone is reacting to each other.

Luminescent banners hang from the walls as late 80s House drifts through the area. Most of the girls are in here waving their hands to the DUFF. I leave them to it and head into the Jungle arena. The dark sounds almost stifling thought. Pull out the gear and quickly roll a spliff, hand it finished to Biggie, before rolling another for myself. Let the first inhalation go down quick, then another one, slower this time, easier. Me a 28-gun bad boy. The beats rolling over me, faster and more insistent, dark and dangerous, nebulous, underwater, slowing down time and interpretations. The crowd is excited and I get up onto my toes and let the sounds of now run around me as the lyrics stomp into indecipherability as the bass is turned up and the speakers start to distort the sound. Push my lighter into the air and flash it, feeling a wave of empathy as others flash theirs. We are all part of the same tribe. Drum and bass binds us together.

Guerrilla dance, guerrilla musicality, coming from anywhere, taking what is needed, taking what is required. No waiting for copyright clearance, none of this bullshit displaying respect for a tune. Out to show that if someone comes up with the original tune, you can go one better by reinventing it, redesigning it. Just jumping in there to create a new version, upgrading it. Making it better. This is the end of the 20th Century, the edge of infinity. 21st Century Fox just around the corner. Sample here, timestretch there, loop a beat, change the pitch on that guitar riff. Taking technology to its logical apogee. Music manipulated and redefined. Subversive in the extreme.

This is my time, my age, circling within the hearts of darkness waiting for the millennium to overtake me. Waiting for the madness to erupt again, for the fundamentalists to start us down the road to destruction with their no-compromise rantings. Just waiting. Knowing that I will be in the firing line. That I'm going to be one of those shot to pieces. The young always get it in the head. Why should my generation be any different?

But that's all in the future. Right now, right here, I'm dancing, running on the spot, my lighter raised to the ceiling, letting it all hang out. I fear no man, beast or god, for the music surrounds me, makes me strong. Feel the blood thunder in my veins as I reach explosion point, the MC screaming for the rewind, our voices lifted in unison with him. Of the same mind, linked, joined at the heart by the music. Jungle.

Sunday
Outro

"Hail for the rewind. Hail for it."

The Rising

My life, my life, my life. If you look into my life and see what I've seen, sings the radio.
— Roy Ayers; Mary J. — whoever, whatever.

A revolution occurs every so often on the junction of Loughborough, this argument revolves around samples. The day starts as it will end: the Sunday elders pray for their weekly sins, the cabbies sell their greens to make ends, while the beast inspects the natives in this corner of the plantation.

Craig's mind began to spin, slow down, speed up then slow down again as he rose from the dark like a whisper to a scream. *Put my head out of the window*, he thought. The carbon dioxide in the air and the certainty that no one cares made him feel, *I could just kill a man*. Police sirens, Jungle bass echoing through ecosphere, brought reality in like a bad rush. Home is where the hatred is:

homes, white-powdered dreams. Home's a bed-sit above a chip shop with mafioso Greek landlord. He had that dry taste in his mouth, an urge to do, the need to step out, the desire to feel the burning rush of riddim and bass. Phone calls had to be made, venues found, life had found meaning again.

At that moment a call came in. He refused and allowed the answering machine to do its job. He went back to bed feeling in his heart he was winning this war. It had to come as a turnaround, viewing the horizon and seeing a cloud that had been the size of a hand grow. The peaceful road towards high calm and chartless places would be a ghetto dream formed in the smoke of sensi. In this smoke Craig saw the world, felt his itch for cocaine, but Coke isn't it. He wanted to get high 'cause he didn't want to feel poor. The ghetto circumstance was like shit on his shoes, so getting high was all so easy and all too sweet. Falling in love was too long, too hard, drawn out, risky, always painful and short-lived. Things had to change.

Sundays always brought the witnesses of Jehovah to his door, prying into his business, preaching a gospel of one sort or another, a gospel Craig felt today he'd rewrite.

As they pushed the youngest of the group of four to the door, Craig watched through the spy glass waiting to pounce: a sweet girl done up in the glorious Sunday pinks; an ordinary girl, but he knew she was a virgin. Craig made that observation on a basis which reckoned only virgins could play the tambourine in those choirs outside Brixton tube, and she was it, chief tambourine and triangle organist, the one girl at the front singing I'm *saving myself for God*. The shock would be one day they'd meet a hippie who'd say Hello, I'm *the lord*.

She came up to press the buzzer, but before she had a chance he opened the door and began.

— Are there any niggas standing on my door? Let's see: one nigga, a paki and whitey — sorry: whiteys, plural.

At first they didn't know how to take it, but they ignored the statement. To Craig this was a good sign, they were veterans. They began their spiel, begging for souls with loose change and loose minds. Craig waited till they said the key word: God. Then he pounced.

— Let me tell you about God. God was a person, a person from another place. He came to earth, thought he'd settle down. He knew he'd make a fortune here and has been cleaning up every Sunday.

Here they began to look around to see how

the others were taking it. For the most part these upper-brained, these almost pseudo Bible-bashing intellectuals were baffled by the venom of this verbal assault.

— You wanna know the point? I'll tell you.

There was a sign and a look on their faces: a wish they'd never knocked on this door.

— The point is oppression. Yes, oppression. Oppression, suppression and repression of the word, a word God created in order that we further fathom and expand thought.

Craig was speaking in his best tongue and only wearing his best Calvins (Klein).

— Whether the word is *bitch*, *cunt*, *slag*, *whore*, *fuck* or *cum*, they aren't used. Take this word *nigga* for instance, it is only a word yet its violence is tantamount to partition of the Red Sea or Abraham burning the marijuana trees. Or more to the point, God never liked too many people – he only ever spoke to Moses, so what the fuck you talking about?

In fact the Jehovah people were quite relieved when he misquoted scripts from the Bible since they could correct him on his misdemeanours. However, he wasn't stopping.

— Check it, if the Queen would just go on TV

and say N*igga*, *nigga*, *nigga*, *nigga*, the world would be an honest place. Maybe some little black kid won't have to cry because now niggas are niggas by appointment of the Queen.

As a saving grace the posse of Jehovah's Witnesses made a quick enquiry as to whether a Mr Black lived there and asked him if he'd like a touch from God in a copy of the *Watchtower*. Craig smiled and said yes, saying in a whisper:

— You know, God touches me . . . at night . . . it is quite marvellous.

Knowing full well a Mr Black didn't live there, they quickly left, but still Craig stepped out in the street and shouted.

— Niggas, jews, whiteys! If there's hell below we're all gonna go, and anyway we all know who the devil is, the devil's the white man!

He stood there in the street and took a look around. Kids were riding their bikes while parents stole glances to keep track of their young. The trees stood under the gaze of concrete, the clouds made fleeting visits. He began to laugh.

— It's all good, it's all good when you are who you are, it's all good.

Jungle Fever

I lie in my bed, sated – the night over, the music pulsing around me – and wonder, What happens now? Deep thoughts for one so young. But it must be done sooner or later. I lie here contemplating my ceiling, wondering what I was placed here to do, why I am the way I am and when, if ever, will I change. I contemplate this and other things while I try to get off to sleep, my energy level still too high for the non-action that is sleep. The fever's in my blood and I can't get it out. Lie here and think, roll, twist, turn. Think about my life, the high times and the bass lines and know that if I had the chance to do it all again I'd start smoking a lot sooner, get blunted more often and try like hell to avoid Cassie. Peace.

Helicopter

**Writing my name and graffiti on the
wall.**

Greeting old walkways with darkness, a
crude affection takes shape, a soul silhouette in
the sun, voices drift through the concrete,
screams of children racing through the column.
Home was once an estate, a mile-high, mile-long
tombstone.

A smell conjures a feeling, a face emerges
from the shadows, a face Craig used to know well
(time takes its toll in the Ghetto), a pram, a
young face, she was once Mary and he was
Joseph and then there were only six years in
their lives. He would smile and share some
words but he's in then out.

Craig's mother called, she said *Let's not wait till
the waters run dry*. She meant, let's talk. The stairs
smell, the sun shines yet nothing can warm up

this tomb, not even the fires of hell which day by day draw closer to this estate. She said, *waters run dry*. Craig listened to that message over and over again, hearing her use those words, hearing her voice uneasily speak into a machine, hoping to reach her only son.

Number 30, Craig was surprised but not shocked to find a metal grill guarding the door, he knocked and there she stood. The smell of home embraced him, the warmth, this home, this tomb, in this city, on this island in Babylon.

It was good to come home though he could never stay, he held her and hugged for all the love she had. There was Reggae in the air and a crowd of aunts asking:

— Cynthia, is that Craig? My, isn't he handsome?

— What are you doing now?

— Have you got a girlfriend?

— I used to bath you.

He never understood what they meant by I *used to bath you* and so they go on. He just smiles and looks at his many pictures that litter the room and hopes they'll get their teeth into something else. Cynthia rests herself and the

High Council of Women Elders begins. Craig still stands, it feels like an interaction and it seems Craig has no rights: she wants Craig to settle down, they explain his fate if he doesn't change *the error of his ways*. It would seem they care but they never understand. He's accused of *white girls, smoking, dreads, blasphemy, disrespect* and Jungle. One aunt stands and does some dance and they fall about laughing. The phone rings, another aunt answers the phone, she knows who it is, she tells them to come down, she puts the phone down and together they go for the kill, they tell Craig in no uncertain terms his life will amount to nothing if he carries on his current way of life. They say, there are pretty black girls and jobs, they talk of a good life, a life they've never had, always dreamt they'd find, but have now sent their wishes to God who will reply when they die. Craig agrees, he wants what they have all their lives prayed for, but know less how to get it and keep it in a lifetime. He promises, he lies, he lies a big lie, he says what they want to hear. He tells a joke and all's settled this time.

The tempo switches, Marvin Gaye gets a rotation.

Whats goin' on?
What's happenin' brother?
Flying high.

Out come the yam, ripe banana, rice and peas, chicken, Vimto and sarsaparilla, the best plates and glasses. In this home there's love and all is well. Marvin sings:

> *Can I go to a place where good feelings await me?*
> *Self-destruction's in my hand.*

He knows the sufferings of the black man, he knew them well.

As all settle, someone knocks on the door, someone gets up. Craig makes a move for the wine, Craig goes to fetch a bottle opener but instead finds his past. He finds a shadow of a smile and a face that is the very essence of all Angelito's negroes.

— Hello.

— Hello.

— If I'd know you were here I'd never have come . . . I came to see your mum.

— Well, yeah, thanks, she's in the sitting room.

They were only children when they first met, when they first found love, when they first made love.

Anna's Song

Glancing from face to face, conversation to conversation, scrutinising every face and movement in the room with a smile of spiritual care, she noticed Craig's stare, eyeing her every which way. In a moment she panicked, neither one had overcome their feelings and neither one dealt with them, they broke up 'cause Craig was excited by the new world he touched. His was and always will be the pleasure principle, the pursuit which left him one day facing the world alone and unhappy, only finding salvation in the pipe, lying low in the jungle. She got up and held Craig's mother. Cynthia loved Anna, a love Craig could never understand, but felt perhaps it was like his mother wanted to play with his toys, he found this analogy enough to keep tame his jealousy.

— My, how the black girl grown.

She had found strength as a woman and at last

she commanded Craig's respect. For the most part of the day they rapped, the enigma she called Craig was to her Marvin Gaye's music personified, since her first love was music.

Special Dedication

My precious love, I built this garden for us. That was the beginning of a poem which Craig once believed in but never in his years did he believe that any one love in his lifetime could be so real. In that close quiet they'd hug, pull back, look into each other's eyes and smile. His mind and body was sure, the air around them danced with little angels, their spirits produced an enviable charge, with this love, their world in their eyes was clear, pure and innocent, the concrete tombs were wombs and God lived among us, from the cradle to the grave. *Sister Love*, his first Blue Note; his Chocolate City product, his own caramel flow of loving Jazz rain, liquid chaos washing, baptising the streets and his soul.

— Talk to me, she says.

He says nothing, then:
— Will I cry for friends lost?

She seemed surprised by this, but she knew the overwhelming odds that his life had to face, she knew he was lucky to reach 21. She said nothing and held him closer.

— Always, things you see in your mind are never as they were.

She kept quiet, not to disturb, to listen, not listen, agree, hold, smell, kiss, looking all the time into their hearts, setting that agenda that will bring them inspiration. Overcoming their fears and weaknesses with words of comfort, overcoming with reassurances, overcoming those many lonely nights.

— You say you want someone to love, you say you want someone, but Craig are you ready?

His reply was sincere.
— I ain't been nowhere since I had you.

She didn't believe that one phrase could wash away those many nights that had brought with them pain. Yet in one instant, the world had turned.

The radio sits at the other end of the room, Craig puts it on, turns the volume down. She wants to hear Leroy Hudson, he wants to hear 105.3 FM. He decides on 105.3 FM and that's final. The MC shouts – Do *you like it*? and replies –

We *love it*. A deep underwater rhythm begins to pound, this is where life begins and where life ends. – We *rock to it*! the DJ shouts: – Yeah, *yeah, yeah, yeah*! The confines of the room burst open and quietly the Jungle beats, this time, in the dark they feel for each other, as if blind, they find their way round each other's bodies. Making love like the first time, making love to last, her eyes slowly open, her brown pupils look to the window and see the stars, she dreams their destiny and Craig following her look sees the moon and dreams of cool blue nights filled with love. They touched each other, touching in each other what each other wanted touched. Craig felt and felt her whole.

Fight Gravity

*T*he sun sets on the dirty streets, neon heat gives little warmth to the cold truth. The facts are bare, nothing lies in the street, if only to then be blinded by people walking on their own two feet.

— Tell the peoples! *sings the man,* as heads rise from the underground in Brixton, facing a barrage of noise, the darkness, their thoughts. Tell them there's a way, a new way to live. In the belly of Babylon you forget where you're from, you forget Zion.

— Don't be afraid! *sings the man.* All fear is is fear itself. To remove that cloud that stands between your self and the sun, between love, life and power you have to know where you're from and keep doing whatever sets you free.

From early in Craig's years he knew that man-a-man on the street did not have to be abnormally sensitive to be worn down to a cutting edge by the incessant, gratuitous and humiliating danger they faced every day, all day. He had been well conditioned by his environment to believe *not take his culture too seriously. Now things had changed, here was something he could believe in.*

So while people in this city will have enough to do in learning how to accept and love themselves as well as each other, when they have done this, which will not be today or the tomorrow promised yesterday, the joy lost in hate and found in love will be found in the youth, the youts from the deepest, darkest heart of Jungle.

What's real? In all, where is reality? Time works as we spin, what goes around comes around. When the riddim beats our hearts into propulsion, driving us closer together, forging a new consciousness in the heat of the dancehall, we come back, our intentions are with love and as the riddim hits hard no one feels pain.

In the streets things are plain, clearly advertised and clearly defined, everyone knows their rights. Here you've got to live, hustle, find a gimmick, a trade and fast, before you get caught and like cattle fodder eaten, shited and left to the earth. This was the crew, each one would teach one. METH, Q, BIGGIE AND CRAIG.

Monday Morning: Jimmy Crack Corn

Listen to the minds, hear what they say: nothing, nothing, on the morning train. ascension, achingly, adrenalin, ahh, ain't, alot, amanda, amethysts, angelou, aquamarine, aretha, armani, arse, arselicker, aryan, atcha, attak, aways, baaaaaaaaaaabee, back's, balham, bandana, basslike, bassline, batman's, battersea, beatbox, beatles, beatifically, bec, bev, bicep, biggie'll, bjork, blag, blige, bloodclot, blowback, bm, bollocks, boonies, boxers, bpm, brats, brixton, brockie, bubblegum, bullshitting, bwoy, call's, camden, cassie, castle's, caz, cd, cept, chillout, chugg, cigs, clapham, clapham's, cock's, commentary, conversation, cortina, cortinas, croydon, crucifixionlike, cunt, da, dalston, dancefloor, darkcore, dat, daytona, daz, dazs, dear's, djing, djn, djs, dodgy, donny, duff, duffs, dulwich, duvet, eco, eeeeing, elvin, em, emily, erika, everythime, ex, existers, featherlite, feeli, fella, fever's, flav, flava, flipside, flynn, fm, foghorns, fozzie, frictionless, fridge, fu, fuck, fucked, fucker, fuckin, fucking, fuckrees, funkin, g's, gales, garms, gaye, gettin, ghettoised, gipper, giri, girlfriends, globulous, goliaths, gook, gotta, grooverider, guestlist, haagen, halen, hammersmith, hangin, hardcore, harley, harman, harassing, hathaway, havin, headfuck, heathrow, hefting, heres, herne, hilda, hmmmm, hmmmming, hmmmmmmm, han, holl, honey's, hounslow, hughie, hummah, hyperspace, i'd, i'm, i'ma, ian, icaus, iceni, ii, ikea, ikea's, illuminous, im, inbetween, indecipherability, info, innie, insubstantiality, intro, it'sa, itv, jamms, jap's, jeeping, jelica, jetness, jodeci, johnathon, jolson, jordan, juddering, jungle, JUNGLIST, kani, kardon, kennington, kensington, kermit, kickin, kingsize, kramer, la, langston, lauren, laurent, lazerdrome, lazerdrome's, leeds, lettin, lewisham, limpish, linford, ll, luton, lycra, macs, mage, mandy, mansell, marantz, markins, marlboro, maximus, mc, mccree, mebe, megadrive, megatron, merc, metamorphosised, meth, meth's, mic, micky, midian, minefield, mirrorlike, mobiles, moistness, morphs, moschino, motorbikes, nottos, mph, mtv, mum's, mumblings, munchies, muppet, musketeers, musklike, nah, naw, neck's, ngowurah, nigel, nigerian, nigga, niggas, nintendo, noo, now's, nuff, nutter, nuttin, o'neal, ogden, ooooooo, orion's, outie, outro, outta, overdrafts, patball, paulette, peckham,

peckham's, perfection, picard, pimlico, pistoning, plz, po, ponce, practised, prams, proteck, puffhead, pussy, putney, puttin, q'll, q's, quentin, ragga, ralphie, ramblings, rantings, ravers, receptors, recharger, reebok, reggie, reinventing, revolver's, ricky, riff, rizla, rizla's, roach, rollin, roughass, royce, rpm, rubbishness, rumblism, rupert, sade, scamming, schott, schwarzenigga, secs, sega, semesterisation, sensi, separatist, sexual, shaquille, shekels, shit's, shite, shoppers, sibilants, skool, sl, slickly, slipmat, slipout, slippin, smokers, smokin, snapple, somalians, somewhere's, sony, soulmate, soundbites, soundstage, spasming, spliff, spliff's, spliffs, sprites, st, starlike, std, stockwell, streatham, streetfighter, sunray, supplications, swaying, sweeney, swingin, sydenham, tai, talkin, tannoy, tanya, tarantino, tck, technics, techno, tekno, tenner, tess, thang, thanx, throwin, timestretch, toke, tonite, touch, tractability, trafalgar, tuff, tulse, turfed, tv, two's, tyres, uni, unitisation, unless, unmoving, unseeingly, unwrinkle, vans, vauxhall, versa, versace, vess, virtua, vs, vu, wack, wais, wanked, wanking, wanking's, wankmeister, wanna, wannabe, wearin, welling, wembley, whatcha, whinee, whirr, whispery, wid, wilds, winder, windscreen, wipers, workload, wraiths, wrestler, wuz, ya, yasmina, yell's, yep, yessir, yo, yorkshireman, yr, yves, zippo. Note: F*uck* and I*t* are key words in the Ghetto vocab.

Jungle (The Apotheosis)

1. an equatorial forest area with luxuriant vegetation, often almost impenetrable. 2. any dense or tangled thicket or growth. 3. a place of intense competition or ruthless struggle for survival.

JAMES T. KIRK a.k.a. Eddie Otchere, is twenty-one years old and was born at the age of sixteen in London. Immediately he began writing experimental literature based on the popular *Reader's Wives* columns of various top-shelf magazines. Among his many talents James boasts that he is one of the few boys in the country to be able to ejaculate six feet into the air. He now feels that after writing this novel he can accomplish his three life long ambitions: to become a drugs baron, a porno star and a photographer.

TWO FINGERS a.k.a. Andrew Green, is twenty-one years old and was born in St. Thomas's hospital on the South Bank of the river Thames. His teen years consisted of a healthy diet of TV, comics, video games and a little bit of school. Two Fingers aims to make *Junglist* into a full length feature film with all action in-yer-face hardcore shit going on in it. Currently studying film in Newcastle he says the only problem with living on Tyneside is that everyone thinks he's Andy Cole. Look out for more scripts, short stories and goings on over the next few years . . .

Junglist is their first novel. Not their last.